Stage Fright

Longarm had no doubt. This was for real. For the Dodger, too—as Longarm now thought of him. Robbing a stage was one thing. But cold-blooded murder was something else again. The Dodger now found himself out of his depth. He mopped his brow nervously.

"Nervous?" Longarm asked.

"Hell, no," he lied. "I ain't nervous."

"Wouldn't blame you if you were. Killin' a man in cold blood ain't all that easy."

"You don't think so?"

"I know so."

"I'll get used to it."

"If you hang with them two over there much longer," said Longarm, "you'll have to get used to it . . ."

Also in the LONGARM series
from Jove

⇥ TABOR EVANS ⇤

LONGARM

AND THE OUTLAW SHERIFF

J

JOVE BOOKS, NEW YORK

LONGARM AND THE OUTLAW SHERIFF

A Jove Book/published by arrangement with
the author

PRINTING HISTORY
Jove edition/July 1989

ISBN: 0-515-10061-7

Jove books are published by The Berkley Publishing Group
200 Madison Avenue, New York, New York 10016.
The name "JOVE" and the "J" logo
are trademarks belonging to Jove Publications, Inc.

PRINTED IN THE UNITED STATES OF AMERICA

10 9 8 7 6 5 4 3 2 1

Chapter 1

Longarm was feeling too good to hurry. He had spent most of the previous evening in a smoke-filled room at the Windsor Hotel, cursing his cards until a generous and warmhearted widow woman had rescued him from his folly. Now, at the beginning of a new day, he was tramping across the Colfax Avenue bridge on his way to the office.

Dressed in a brown tweed frock coat and pants, the U.S. deputy marshal loomed somewhat spookily in the early morning light. He was better than six feet tall and moved with the ease of a giant cat, his strides eating up the ground faster than lesser men could manage at a steady trot. His lean, rawboned features had been cured to a deep brown by the elements, and if it were not for the gunmetal blue of his wide-set eyes, the tobacco-leaf color of his hair, and the flaring upthrust of his longhorn mustache, he might easily have been mistaken for a Cheyenne warrior.

He ran his palm over his chin. The rasping sound that resulted seemed loud enough to wake the hobos sleeping under the bridge. The widow woman had not had a razor handy, so he had forgone his morning shave. He sure as hell needed one, but if he took the time he'd be late. What the hell? He hadn't been on time once in the past week. If Billy Vail took offense and cussed him out, it wouldn't be anything new.

Farther up Colfax Avenue he turned into George Masters's barbershop and saw that George was nearly finished with a customer. The chair was all the way back, the gent's legs propped straight out, a sheet draped over his body. George was patting a steaming hot towel onto the man's face. The only features of the customer's face visible were his flaring, beetling eyebrows. Longarm hung his snuff-brown Stetson on the hat rack, sat down, and pulled a copy of Lesley's *Illustrated Weekly* onto his lap. The paper was unable to capture his interest, however, and he glanced up expectantly as George Masters levered the barber chair back upright and whipped the sheet off his customer's lap in grand style, snapping it loudly.

"Next!" he said, glancing over at Longarm.

The customer with the untidy brows stepped down out of the barber chair and turned to face Longarm, the yawning bore of a Navy Colt aimed at Longarm's gut. From under Lesley's *Illustrated Weekly* the twin muzzles of Longarm's derringer blasted. Two neat holes appeared in the man's vest. The ex-convict Longarm recognized as Jake Barnes dropped his Colt, took a step back and sat back down in the barber chair. He leaned

2

back—but not for a shave and haircut this time.

"My God, Longarm!" Mopping his face with a handkerchief laced with bay rum, George peered down at the dead man's slack face, still shiny and pink from his recent shave. "When I saw him come up with that cannon, I couldn't believe it. Who the hell is he?"

"Jake Barnes. A prizefighter once, before he turned safecracker. I sent him to Yuma a few years back."

George groaned. "I should've known!"

"What do you mean?"

"A week ago this gent came in and asked if you ever dropped in for a shave. Said he was an old friend. He's been coming in here every morning since." George shook his head. "I'm sorry, Longarm. I should've realized. A man in your line of work don't *have* no friends."

"Well, let's say not this early in the morning."

Their discussion was broken off by the arrival of Jerry O'Leary, a uniformed member of the Denver police. He pushed through the crowd that had gathered outside and stepped into the shop. One look at the dead man slacked in the barber's chair and he pulled up, sighing.

Then he recognized Longarm.

"I see you're back in form, Custis."

"Yep, Jerry. Sorry about that."

"Oh, I guess maybe you got a right to use your gun if you want."

"That's right generous of you."

O'Leary moved past Longarm and looked carefully down at the dead man. Then he glanced over at the still-perspiring George. "And that's a nice close shave you gave him, George. Didn't miss a hair, looks like."

3

Then he looked back at Longarm. "This dead man an acquaintance of yours, is he?"

Longarm nodded. "I recognized him soon's I came in. When I took off my hat, I palmed my derringer and kept it ready under the weekly I was reading."

"That's real tricky. He got a name?"

"Jake Barnes. Just got out of Yuma, I reckon—and came all the way up here just to pay his respects. That's his Navy Colt on the floor."

The roundsman bent, picked it up, and shoved it down behind his tight black leather belt. "You'll have to come down to the station house and help me make out a report, Custis. As usual."

"Sure thing, O'Leary. But let's get a move on. Billy Vail is going to cloud up and rain all over me if I come in too late."

The morning mists had cleared away completely by the time Longarm left the police station and resumed his walk up Colfax Avenue. The gilded dome of the Colorado State House gleamed in the bright sunlight. At Cherokee and Colfax, he swung around the corner and headed for the Federal Building, mounted the steps, and elbowed his way through the downstairs lobby, which was filled with officious-looking dudes. He climbed the marble staircase and made his way to a large oak door whose gold-leaf lettering read, UNITED STATES MARSHAL, FIRST DISTRICT COURT OF COLORADO.

Turning the knob, he shouldered his way inside and approached the bespectacled clerk pounding the keys of a newfangled engine they called a typewriter.

"Billy in?" Longarm inquired. The question was only

4

a formality. Of course the marshal was in. Where else would he be?

"Marshal Vail's been lookin' for you, Longarm," Henry warned. "You better go right in."

Longarm knocked lightly, pushed open the door and entered Vail's office. Marshal Billy Vail—a round, balding, pink-cheeked older man rapidly going to seed —was pawing through a blizzard of paper and assorted reports piled high on his desk. His IN and OUT baskets were overflowing. Glancing up at Longarm, the marshal sighed wearily, then leaned back in his swivel chair.

"Damn it, Longarm, where the hell you been?"

"It's a long story."

"I'll bet it is!" He tipped his head to look at Longarm more closely. "And what in blazes do you mean coming in looking like that? You need a shave. What's the matter? Don't you own a razor? Just what is it that makes you think this here federal office is eager to employ unshaven louts who sleep till noon?"

Longarm glanced at the banjo clock on the wall. It was a little past ten o'clock. "Never gave it much thought, Chief."

"All right, damn it! Where you been?"

Longarm sat down in the morocco leather chair beside Vail's desk and, placing his Stetson on the corner of it, took out a cheroot and lit it.

"Quit stalling," Billy Vail demanded.

Longarm leaned back in the soft leather chair. He had a theory about Billy Vail. Billy always seemed to have a hair across his ass because he was jealous of Longarm, and maybe the other deputies as well. While he, the U.S. federal marshal, was trapped behind a desk, Longarm and the other operatives were free to

5

roam over the mountains, plains, and deserts of this vast Western land. Billy Vail had once done the same thing, and missed it mightily. Billy had whupped and corraled more *bandidos*, renegade redskins, and assorted killers and highwaymen than most of the men currently on his payroll.

With his cheroot lit, Longarm leaned back and told Vail all about his visit to George Masters's barbershop, and to the local police station that followed. When he had finished, Vail leaned back in his swivel chair and shook his head in pure wonderment.

"You mean to say you recognized the son of a bitch by his *eyebrows*?"

"You never saw those eyebrows, Chief. They were curly and wild, stood out like small wire brushes—very individual."

"That so?"

"Take yours, now. They're thin, gray at the edges, but dark enough in the center. I'd recognize them anywhere."

"All right. Cut it out, now. You're just showing off." He chuckled. "It sure is a caution what you won't go through, Longarm, just so you don't have to show up on time."

"It is at that."

Longarm's story had taken the wind out of Vail's sails. He had no good reason to complain of Longarm's tardiness. Not this morning, at any rate. With a deep sigh, he glanced briefly down at his cluttered desk, then up at Longarm.

"What say we get the hell out of here and go across to that new diner? I need a cup of coffee, and maybe you could use a little nourishment yourself."

6

"You mean all is forgiven?"

"I'm invitin' you to some coffee and doughnuts, and it's on me. What the hell more do you want?"

Longarm grinned and held up his hands in token surrender.

"Besides," Vail continued, "I got an assignment I want to talk over with you. But not here."

Vail moved out from behind his desk, lifted his hat off the hat rack, and was a step ahead of Longarm when they left his office.

A few minutes later, a cup of coffee in front of him, Vail looked across the table and shook his head. "It still beats the shit out of me how you could identify a man just from his eyebrows. I never heard of such a thing."

Longarm shrugged modestly and sipped his coffee. "What's this assignment you got for me, Chief?"

After taking a moment to assemble his thoughts, Vail said, "Some years ago, Custis, I used to ride with a gent named Tom Billings. He was a good kid, and a lot younger than me. I taught him what I could. He caught on fast. An apt pupil, you might say."

He paused to sip his steaming coffee, then reached for one of the doughnuts they had ordered.

"Came a time Tom and me went our separate ways. He dropped out of sight and I didn't hear a thing about him for a couple of years. Then word got back to me that he'd joined a wild outfit that held up a Wells Fargo office in North Dakota. They were after a federal gold shipment, but they didn't get far. The gang was surrounded in an old barn. The barn caught fire, and those that didn't get fried took a fatal dose of lead poisoning. But Billings got away. That was what I heard, anyway."

7

"When was this?"

"Near five years ago."

Longarm nodded and waited.

"Well," Vail resumed, "I just got word from Washington. Seems that Billings has turned up in a small town west of here. Rimrock. He's the sheriff, for Christ's sake."

"And you want me to go after him."

"I do and I don't."

"You want to explain that?"

"Custis, I don't think Tom had anything to do with that Wells Fargo heist. The kid I knew was honest clear through. One thing you can't change—the way I see it—and that's the quality of a man's backbone. The way I figure it, one of the gang's dying members fingered Tom to even an old score." Vail shrugged fatalistically. "But my feelin's don't cut no ice with Washington. Tom's still wanted for his part in that North Dakota heist, and I have to send someone after him."

"So you're sending me?"

"I know you, Custis. I trust you. You won't just rush in there and start blasting. What I'm hoping is you'll take your time and ask around some before you make a move. Keep your badge out of sight and see if you can find out if that damned outlaw was telling the truth when he implicated Tom in that gold heist. Think you could do that, Custis?"

"I'll do what I can," Longarm promised. "No reason why I can't ask around first, take my time before making any move. But that'll take time, Billy."

Billy leaned his head back against the booth, relieved. "Well, I sure as hell can't ask for more than that. Take all the time you need. And thanks, Custis."

"When do I leave?"

"Today. You'll take a train to Gunnison, but after that you'll be boarding a stage to Rimrock. Hell, you might be back inside a week."

"That's not how it usually turns out, Chief."

"I know," Vail admitted. "Now why don't you go and get that shave? When you get back, I'll have your travel vouchers ready—and what I hope you won't need."

"What's that?"

"A federal warrant for Tom's arrest."

Chapter 2

Relaxing on the Rimrock Hotel veranda, his chair tipped back, Longarm watched Sally Henderson pause at the head of the steps to stare impatiently across at the Wells Fargo Express office. At the moment four men, straining like draft horses, were hauling the coach out of the carriage shed. They were struggling mightily and their progress was painfully slow.

One of the coach's axles had supposedly buckled, and the coachmen had been working on it since the night before, delaying the departure to Mountain City until this morning. It was now close to nine o'clock. The delay had been considerable, and Longarm did not blame Sally Henderson for her impatience.

Longarm had traveled to Rimrock with her, sitting directly across from her in the creaking, swaying coach. A few sudden lurches had brought them perilously close to embracing. He had tried to strike up a conversation

11

with her, but she had coolly rebuffed his advances. Nevertheless, she had admitted to having come all the way from Boston, and seemed quite proud of this fact. Longarm figured her for a schoolmarm and lost no sleep over his rebuff. Schoolteachers from the East were tough and formidable creatures, seldom easily won over—even when it was something they wanted themselves.

Tall, commanding in presence, Sally was a handsome woman with sharp blue eyes under wide, arching brows. She was wearing a navy blue dress with a stylishly trim waist, and skirts that brushed the insteps of her patent leather shoes. She kept her abundant auburn curls wound in a tight bun under her straw boater.

She looked away from the express office. Her eyes caught Longarm's. She smiled slightly. Pushing himself upright, Longarm walked over and touched his hat brim to her.

"Hope you had a pleasant night, Miss Henderson."

"I did," she replied coolly. "The bedroom was surprisingly clean, the view of the mountains perfectly splendid."

"This surprised you?"

"This is a dirty, slovenly wilderness, Mr. Long. Inhabited for the most part by aborigines and criminals. Both of whom are invariably extremely dirty. Of course I was surprised."

Longarm chuckled. She wasn't off by much and he liked her spirit. He glanced across the street at the stagecoach still being laboriously hauled from the shed. "Looks like they fixed up the coach. You'll be on your way soon."

"I sincerely hope so. This delay has been most provoking. But I must confess"—she sighed—"that I am not looking forward to another jolting ride over this precipitous land. Are you remaining here in Rimrock, Mr. Long?"

"Yes."

"Why ever would you do such a thing? This is such a gaunt, dusty town. There aren't even paved roads or sidewalks."

"And very little indoor plumbing."

"Please, Mr. Long!"

"Sorry."

"You never did tell me your business, Mr. Long."

"That's right, ma'am, I didn't."

Politely doffing his hat to her, Longarm descended the veranda steps and threaded through the traffic to the express office. The night before, aroused by the constant hammering coming from the repair shop, he had gone to the window in his room and glimpsed a canvas-covered wagon pulling in. What had alerted Longarm at once was the great difficulty the powerful horses seemed to be experiencing as they hauled the wagon up the short wooden ramp that led into the repair shed. There had obviously been a lot more going on inside that shed than anyone was willing to admit.

Longarm mounted the express office steps. The stagecoach driver—the same man who had driven them through the mountains to Rimrock—stepped out onto the porch and planted himself in front of Longarm. He was a husky, leathery faced man in his late forties or early fifties, with the stub of a cigar stuck in his wide, bulldog mouth. His shoulders and forearms were powerful, his thick waist as solid as a tree trunk. Since his name was MacDonald, everyone called him Mac.

"Howdy, mister," he said. "You lookin' to buy a ticket?"

"Nope. I got to where I was going when we pulled in here last night."

"Glad to hear that. What can I do for you?"

"I was wondering about all that racket last night. You fellers sure did a lot of hammering and sawing just to fix a single axle."

"That's your opinion, is it?"

Longarm nodded.

"Well, this is a free country. You got a right to believe any damn thing you want."

"I didn't mean to rile you none," Longarm replied easily, smiling. "It just sounded to me like your carpenters were working hard enough to build a new stagecoach."

MacDonald shifted impatiently under Longarm's easy stare. "We found a few other things to repair. After all, I don't want to risk no breakdowns on the way to Mountain City."

"Well, I can sure understand that," Longarm said. "Good morning, sir."

Longarm descended to the street. The evasive response to his questioning was just what he had expected. If that night crew had stashed something valuable somewhere on the stage, there was no reason in the world why MacDonald should admit that to Longarm—or to anyone else. But Longarm now had no doubt at all that this was indeed what they had done.

In Gunnison two days earlier, he had heard talk of something valuable—a gold shipment—on its way from the Denver mint. It had come on the train, some said, the same one Longarm had taken. The gold's destination was the booming copper mine in the mountains west of Rimrock. Because of the staggering inflation in the town, the miners had come to distrust the value of paper currency and were on strike until they were paid in gold. This shipment was supposed to be it.

It all fitted in nicely. That wagon Longarm had seen the night before entering the repair shed must have contained the gold that was now hidden on the stage, more than likely secreted under a false floor.

As Longarm strode down the street toward the sheriff's office, he found himself anxious to meet Billy Vail's old sidekick. But at the same time he was aware that he might well be disappointed. According to the deputy, whom he had spoken to the night before, Billings had ridden to Mountain City in order to swear in two new deputies. The two he had sworn in a month earlier had managed to get their guts blown out in a high-stakes poker game. Longarm was hoping that Billings might possibly have ridden back in earlier that morning.

Longarm was passing in front of the town's general store when a pretty young lady in her late twenties came out lugging a sack of flour. He halted in his tracks, took the flour sack from her with a smile and dropped it onto the bed of her flatbed wagon, alongside the rest of the provisions already loaded. She thanked him with a weary smile, then leaned back against the wagon and wiped her brow with the back of her forearm.

Her name was Jenny Wills. Recently widowed, she was now running by herself a ranch left to her by her deceased husband. She had driven her flatbed into Rimrock the day before and had stayed overnight at the hotel. While he was getting acquainted with her little boy, Joshua, in the hotel lobby that morning, Longarm had introduced himself to her. Her beauty lay mostly in the warmth of her expressive eyes and in the calm, almost serene cast to her plain features.

"Let me give you a hand, Jenny," Longarm said.

"Thank you, Mr. Long. That would be a great help. I *am* anxious to get going."

Longarm worked smoothly with the store clerk, and between them—and little Josh—they soon had the flatbed loaded. Jenny lifted her six-year-old daughter, Annie, up onto the wagon seat and turned to Longarm.

"Thank you so much, Mr. Long."

"My pleasure," he said. "And be careful. From what you told me this morning, that's a long drive out to that ranch of yours."

"Oh, I've made it safely many times," she assured him, smiling. And before he could reach out to give her a hand up, she climbed swiftly onto the wagon seat beside her daughter. It was clear she savored her independence—or was being very careful not to appear helpless. Probably both.

Josh came out of the store sucking on a peppermint candy stick, his reward, evidently, for helping load the wagon.

"Josh," his mother called, "would you like to show Mr. Long how well you drive the team?"

Josh's eyes widened. "Sure, Ma!"

The peppermint stick protruding from his mouth, Josh scrambled up onto the seat beside his mother. Carefully adjusting the reins to fit his small hands, he slapped them across the team's backs.

"Gee up!"

The two horses started up promptly. With his mother

watching proudly, Josh executed a neat turn, urged his horses to a smart run, and with a wave to Longarm, drove the team past him and out of town.

Smiling, Longarm watched the family disappear, then resumed his walk to the sheriff's office. Entering it, he found the deputy making himself comfortable behind Billings's desk, his hat tipped back off his forehead, his lanky legs crossed on the corner of the desk. His name was Danny. He was a gawky, sandy-haired wisp of a young man, all eagerness and blundering good nature. He reminded Longarm of an eager puppy thrusting his snout into badger holes and hornets' nests. Not much use but a pleasant companion.

"Mornin', mister. Tom ain't back yet."

"I guessed as much." Longarm slumped into the chair beside the desk and took out a cheroot. "Maybe if I want to see him, I should take the stage to Mountain City."

"If you're that anxious."

Longarm scraped a wooden match over the desktop and lit his cheroot.

"He's been gone how long now?"

"I told you. Four days."

"Just when did he think he might be getting back?"

"Now, how the hell should he know that, mister? Mountain City's one helluva place just about now, from what I hear."

"I heard about it in the hotel last night. Seems the miners have gone out on strike."

"Yeah," the deputy agreed. "But before that Mountain City was runnin' wide open. Them miners've invited the devil to join the party, and it looks like he's measurin' the place for a second hell. Could take the sheriff a week, maybe two, to pull himself out of there. On the other hand, he might ride in this afternoon." Danny laced his hands behind his head and smiled smugly at Longarm. "Of course, he ain't in no real hurry to get back. He knows damn well I can handle things here."

"Pretty quiet town, is it?"

"Hell! That's the trouble. Ain't nothin' happened here since a redheaded brat tried to burn his own grandma in the privy."

"When was that?"

"Six years ago."

Longarm got to his feet. "Thanks, Danny."

"You goin' to take that stage to Mountain City?"

"Don't know. I'll have to think on it. Maybe I'll give Billings another day or two, anyway."

"You ain't told me yet why you're so anxious to see the sheriff, mister. What shall I tell him if he shows up?"

"Just tell him I'm a friend of an old friend of his. Just payin' my respects is all."

Danny frowned. Longarm's answer had not told him a damn thing.

Longarm left the sheriff's office and paused for a while on the porch, his gaze settling on the saloon across the street. He was restless. Hanging around Rimrock did not appeal to him. This dusty town was everything Sally Henderson had proclaimed it to be. It was a grim, rock-bound settlement squeezed between harsh mountain walls high in the Rockies. He could just imagine the winters up here, and it was not at all difficult to understand why that homicidal redhead was still remembered after six years—or why he had turned homicidal in the first place.

Longarm descended the jailhouse steps, crossed the street, and shouldered through the batwings into the saloon. The swamper was at work in back and the chairs were still sitting upside down on top of the tables. The lamps over the gaming tables were not burning. Longarm strode over to the bar and distracted the barkeep long enough from his morning inventory to pay for a beer. He took it over to a table in the corner and lifted the chairs off the table, selected one for himself, and sat down, his back to the wall. He was not there long when three more patrons entered, selecting a table near the door. Two were men, the other a young girl. The girl and one of the men appeared to have just ridden in, judging from the white patina of dust that covered them.

Longarm had noticed the taller of the two men the night before in the hotel lobby. At the time he was almost certain he knew the face, but from where? Now he remembered. He had seen that lean, lantern-jawed face on a Wanted poster. The gent's name was Carl Sutter, and he was wanted for more than seven counts of armed robbery.

Without staring at him directly, Longarm studied the man. Sutter looked to be close to forty. His hat was torn, his jacket and Levi's shiny with grime. Indeed, the only item on his person that seemed cared for was the gleaming, well-oiled Peacemaker resting in his oiled holster, something everyone in the hotel lobby had noticed the night before. His long neck and gaunt, unshaven face were dark with caked dirt. Stringy yellow hair hung down in untidy clots, and his eyes burned with a hectic, feverish light.

The other two with Sutter were no bargains either.

The second male was a hoggish, oversized ruffian of

indeterminate age, his eyes resembling raisins stuck in a pan of bread dough. So huge was his belly it flowed out over his gun belt, almost completely hiding it. The girl was in her teens or early twenties. She was so small the barrel of the Navy Colt strapped to her thigh reached clear to her knee. Thick, untidy curls tumbled past her shoulders. Her lips were small, yet full—the lips of a dangerously precocious little girl.

Sutter seemed to be doing all the talking. And while he did so—bent forward over the table, his voice low, conspiratorial—the girl leaned back in her chair and sipped her whiskey, her cold, calculating eyes studying Sutter with a mixture of amusement and contempt. She seemed to be barely tolerating these two men while waiting for someone better to come along.

Watching the three of them, Longarm found it impossible not to think of that gold shipment that had been so laboriously hidden on the stage the night before, and that would soon be on its way to Mountain City. Of course, there might be nothing to his suspicions. These three did not have to be in town simply because of that shipment. They probably knew nothing about it. Hell, he was guessing about it himself. Abruptly, he told himself to shut up. There wasn't any doubt in his mind what these three were up to.

This trio of gunslicks were fixing to hit the Mountain City stage.

Finishing his beer, Longarm got up from his table for a refill. While the barkeep filled his stein, the three got up from their table and left the saloon. Longarm took his beer to a window and, sipping it, watched them. Sutter had already mounted a powerful chestnut. Without a glance back at the two, he lifted his mount to a lope and rode out of town.

The fat man and the girl, meanwhile, trudged up the street toward the Wells Fargo office. Already the hostlers were backing the teams into the coach's traces. As Longarm watched, an extra brace of horses was led out of the horse barn. In a moment the fat man and the girl had reached the express office and were mounting the steps to it, obviously to purchase tickets for the ride to Mountain City.

Longarm had seen enough.

He finished his beer, slapped the empty stein onto a table, and strode from the saloon. Hell, he had no choice in the matter. He was going to have to warn the stationmaster.

Chapter 3

"You mind saying that over again?" the Wells Fargo agent said, frowning up at Longarm.

Longarm had asked to speak to the agent privately, but the man had remained behind the low railing without inviting Longarm into his private office. The agent was a lean, sallow man wearing a green eyeshade, sleeve garters and wire-rimmed spectacles. His hugely magnified eyes swam behind his thick glasses like fish in a bowl.

"I think maybe you ought to hire some armed riders to follow behind this stage."

"Follow behind?"

"That's right. And keep maybe a half mile or so back."

"Now, why in hell would I want to do that?"

"You want me to spell it out?"

"I sure do, mister."

"I think this stage runs a pretty good chance of being held up between here and Mountain City."

"Now what in hell makes you think that, mister?"

"We have to talk out here, do we?"

The express agent frowned. "In here, then."

The agent held open the gate for Longarm, who stepped through it, then followed the agent into his inner office. Sitting back down on the corner of his desk, the Wells Fargo agent cocked his head at Longarm.

"So talk, mister."

Longarm told him about the trio he had just seen in the saloon. He told him he suspected one of the men was a wanted highwayman and that this was the one who had ridden out of town while the other two had purchased tickets for Mountain City.

"That all you got?"

"That, and the fact you got a load of gold hidden somewhere on that stage."

"Now what gave you that crazy idea?"

"You deny it?"

"Why should I admit to something as crazy as that? And what's your interest in this, mister? Who the hell *are* you, anyway?"

Longarm took a deep, unhappy breath. In order to make this agent take him seriously, he would have to reveal who he was. It would make things a lot simpler for everyone. But he had promised Vail that he would not let Billings or anyone else in Rimrock know who he was or what he was about until he had thoroughly checked out Sheriff Billings.

"Forget it," Longarm said. "Looks like I'll be buying a ticket for Mountain City."

Longarm turned on his heels and led the way out of the agent's office.

As Longarm climbed onto the stage not long afterward, Sally Henderson glanced at him in some surprise. After all, he had told her not so long before that he was staying in Rimrock. But she said nothing on his change of plans and edged her supple frame into the corner of the coach beside him. At the same time, Longarm noted, she did her best not to look into the eyes of the fat man sitting across from her and the tough, dirty-faced young lady beside him.

There was little doubt in Longarm's mind that he had guessed right. The gun-toting lady was obviously as tough as a horseshoe, her companion too big and too fat to ever have made an honest living.

As the stage rumbled out of Rimrock, Longarm once again noticed how ineffective the stage's leather curtains were. Rolled up to let in what little breeze there might be, they let in choking clouds of dust as well, which stung their eyes and hampered their breathing. Since rolling the curtains back down would only succeed in confining them all inside a rolling, pitching oven, Longarm left the curtains up and leaned back.

With half-closed eyes he surveyed the girl and the fat man. He had heard the fat one call the girl Mary Lou. As he watched her, she stared impudently back at him, perfectly aware that he was studying her in turn. Her bold glance held a sullen, chilling arrogance. Though she was indubitably very young, there was nothing innocent or appealing about her and very little that was feminine. Longarm guessed that this pert, small-boned young girl was following the infamous example of that sad clapped-up whore, Calamity Jane. Despite her tender years, she didn't have far to go, and if she already had a dose, Longarm was pleased it was something he would never be obliged to find out for himself.

Mary Lou had addressed her oversized companion as Dodger. This close up he looked considerably more gross than he had in the saloon. Squeezing painfully into his seat earlier, he had been unable to keep his filthy cotton shirt tucked into his pants. The only item of clothing left to hold back the irresistible tide of his enormous belly was a torn, filthy red undershirt. He was still squirming about in a futile effort to get comfortable. As Longarm watched, the man's red undershirt pulled out from under his belt, revealing a burgeoning patch of white, hairy belly.

Sally Henderson barely managed to muffle her gasp.

The big man looked over at her and made no effort to tuck his undershirt back in. The man reminded Longarm of an enormous toad recently eloped from a hog wallow. He glanced sidelong at Sally Henderson. She had closed her eyes, pretending to sleep—a prudent move. Eventually, the fat man looked away from her.

Longarm relaxed.

Because the stage had left Rimrock two hours late, it did not arrive at the way station until mid-afternoon. The passengers piled out wearily. As soon as he had helped Sally Henderson down, Longarm paused and stretched to his full height to get the stiffness out. Then he headed for the log building.

The way station was serviceable, and little more. The bulk of its furniture was constructed mostly from rough timber and pine logs. A huge fireplace filled the end

26

wall and the rough-hewn shelves above it contained most of the dishes and cast-iron cooking utensils. A huge black iron pot hung from a hook, the potent smell of molasses and beans wafting from it. The only luxury Longarm spied was a most practical one—a hand pump set up beside the sink.

After visiting the privy out in back, Sally entered. Watching her, Longarm noticed at once the depression she felt at the room's primitive interior. He waved to her and caught more than a hint of relief on her face when she saw he was alone at his table. She hurried over and sat down facing him.

"My God! What a filthy place!" She shuddered.

He figured she was referring to the privy and said nothing. There was little either of them could do about that.

The stationmaster's wife hurried over to their table with a pot of fresh coffee. In addition to the coffee, she brought a warmed plate containing hot biscuits, fresh pork and a platter of beans and molasses. The helpings were more than generous, and despite the near heroic weariness etched on her face, the stationmaster's wife served them swiftly, cheerfully, and without complaint.

Across the room, at a table alongside the white-washed wall, Mary Lou and Dodger sat, the big man crouched swinishly over a huge mound of beans and biscuits. Earlier the stage driver and the shotgun messenger, both wolfing down cups of hot coffee, had gone back outside to supervise the change of horses. With impeccable manners Sally ate her plateful of beans, and Longarm was thankful she didn't try to converse with him while eating, a habit that always gave away an Easterner.

His belly satisfyingly full, Longarm pushed his tin plate aside, lit a cheroot, and reached for his coffee. A moment later Sally finished eating and glanced over at Mary Lou and Dodger. She made no effort to conceal her distaste for the pair.

"I was hoping those two would get off here."

"Not much chance of that, I'm afraid."

"I guess not. Looks like they're going all the way to Mountain City."

She took a sip of the coffee and made a face, putting the cup down quickly. She obviously found it much too strong for her tastes. For his part, the coffee had pleased Longarm even more than the beans. After a moment Sally picked the cup up and sipped as much of the coffee as she could get down. Then she pushed the cup aside and looked unhappily about her.

Longarm cleared his throat. "Miss Henderson, I'd be obliged if you'd tell me why you're on your way to Mountain City. And without a proper escort. This here country is most uncongenial for a woman of your sensibilities."

She looked at him for a long moment. "You've noticed, have you?"

"I've noticed."

"Perhaps I do owe you an explanation," she conceded.

"Excuse me, ma'am," Longarm hastened to say, "you don't owe me a thing."

"In that case, I will tell all." A faint smile lit her face. "After all, there's no reason for me to keep it a secret. I'm certainly not ashamed of my reasons for making this grueling trip. It's very simple, Mr. Long. I am coming out here to this godforsaken land to teach school."

"I'd just about figured that."

"Had you now?"

"Miss Henderson, women come out here for three reasons mostly. Their husbands drag them out here because they can't make a go of it back East; they get dumped by the traveling salesmen they ran off with; or they come out here to escape something unpleasant that happened to them back East—like a man."

"A woman compromised, you mean. Or left at the altar."

"Something like that."

She sighed. "My case is somewhat different, but you're not far off, I'm afraid. Tell me, Mr. Long, what makes people think that a woman can be defined only by the man she marries? Is that all a woman is—a mirror image of some fool who thinks he's the Emperor of the Universe because he wears pants?"

"Guess you got me on that," Longarm admitted. "I suppose if you're a lady with a mind of your own, you ain't likely to please most men."

"That's putting it mildly, Mr. Long."

"So one gent in particular couldn't take it, huh?"

"He thought he could. And so did I. But a few days before the wedding, I asked him if I might have my own bank account to use in running the house. I didn't want to have to go running after him for every cent, you see, as my mother had to do with my father."

"Sounds reasonable."

"Yes. . . . Well *he* said that such an arrangement would be out of the question."

Longarm said nothing.

"So then I asked for an allowance to run the house."

"That too sounds reasonable."

She smiled bitterly. "He said *he* would run the house. He said *he* would take care of the bills and handle all the finances. After all, he was the breadwinner. He said he didn't want me to have to worry about such matters. All he expected of me was to bear his children and be a good and faithful wife."

"Did that sound so awful?"

"He didn't let it go at that. He went on to inform me that this was the last time we would discuss the matter. Then he admitted that he had heard I was difficult on such matters, that I was headstrong and harbored queer notions about a woman's place—but he was prepared to marry me anyway and was not going to let such fool notions come between us. Then he leaned forward and kissed me on the forehead."

Longarm smiled. "I'm getting the picture."

"The kiss was the final straw, I suspect," she admitted, smiling wanly. "I acted most horribly, I am afraid. I said terrible things. At any rate, he left and did not come back. He sent his brother for the engagement ring."

"And you threw it at him."

"Yes. I did." She laughed softly. "How ever did you guess?"

Longarm laughed. "It's what I would have done."

"You are most understanding, Mr. Long. Where were you when I needed you? Of course I got no support at all from my parents—or any of my so-called woman friends. When what had happened got around, they were terrified to be seen in my company."

"So now here you are in the middle of this slovenly

wilderness, as you so aptly called it, getting set to teach the unwashed brats of all those aborigines and criminals you mentioned. I guess you showed them."

She looked gloomily around her. "You're so right, Mr. Long. I believe it's called jumping from the frying pan into the fire."

Longarm reached out and patted her hand gently. "Don't weaken now. You've come a long way, and you're close to the end of your journey. Is anyone waiting for you in Mountain City?"

"The members of the school board are expecting me. But I have never met any of them. My correspondence has been solely with the head of the school board, a Mr. Ebenezer Wilson."

Sally Henderson's classical features, cold and unfeeling until this discussion, had by now taken on a quite pleasant animation. Her eyes had lit, and Longarm now found a bright, ironic intelligence reflected in them. From the first, it had occurred to him that she was either a very brave woman to make this trip alone or a very unhappy one.

He was right, it seemed, on both counts.

But he didn't want her to be any more unhappy than she already was, and for that reason considered confiding to her his suspicions concerning Mary Lou and her fat companion. Under the circumstances, it might be a good idea for her to remain back here in the way station and wait for the next stage.

Before he could say anything, however, he heard the stage driver's urgent voice: "Let's go, passengers! Stage pulling out!"

Longarm turned to see MacDonald standing in the

open doorway, a coiled horsewhip in his powerful right hand.

"Thank heaven," said Sally Henderson, getting quickly to her feet. As Longarm followed after her, she turned to him and smiled. "You have no idea how glad I'll be when this trip is over!"

Following her from the way station, Longarm considered for a moment the advisability of pulling her to one side and suggesting she wait for the next stage. But it was too late for that now, he realized. When the other two saw him counseling Sally to leave the coach and remain at the way station, they would know for sure what he suspected—and be forewarned of his intentions to foil them.

Just ahead of him, Sally Henderson lifted her skirts and clambered eagerly into the coach. Longarm followed in behind her. A moment later, Mary Lou and her companion settled into the seat across from them. As the driver and the young shotgun messenger climbed up into the box, Longarm felt the stagecoach rock slightly. The whip cracked and the coach lurched out of the yard.

Slumping back in his seat, Longarm reached under his frock coat to loosen slightly the .44 resting in his cross-draw rig. Then he patted his .44 derringer in his vest's fob pocket, closed his eyes and pretended to sleep.

Mary Lou was amused.

She knew who this bastard was. And why he had shown up at the last minute to take this stagecoach. He was a Pinkerton, sent special to guard this shipment. But it didn't matter. Pinkertons were all fools. Carl was way ahead of them. From the beginning he had been right. The gold shipment they had tracked from Gunnison was just under their feet. The moment she climbed into the stage, she had felt how much higher than normal the stage's floor was.

She looked away from the Pinkerton. When he had first leaned forward to enter the coach, she had noticed the bulge in his watch fob pocket. He was carrying a belly gun in it—a derringer, more than likely—attached to the gold-washed watch chain that hung across his vest. When the time came, she decided, she would ask the Pinkerton what time it was.

She felt Dodger edging his massive rump closer to hers. He reached out slyly and took her left hand. She slipped her six-gun from its holster and, cocking it, pointed the muzzle at his crotch. Dodger pulled his hand away swiftly, cold sweat standing out on his face. She returned her six-gun to her holster, then crossed her arms and leaned back in her seat.

Longarm leaned forward to look out at the bleak, sun-scorched badlands. There had been little rain this summer; some called it a drought. The land was as dry as a bone. The unrelenting sunshine slanted off the rocks and barren slopes, causing him to squint. The only green came from the pines marching up the steep slopes and stippling the buttes and ridges high overhead. He looked away at last and leaned back against the seat again, his eyes slits as he looked across the coach at Mary Lou and the fat man.

Beside him Sally Henderson was still pretending she was asleep. Mary Lou, however, came alert as soon as he leaned back in his seat. Now she was watching him closely, intently. A snake waiting to strike. He opened his eyes all the way and returned her gaze just as boldly.

On the box above, MacDonald was lost in his own thoughts, still puzzling over that tall drink of water who had bought the last ticket to Mountain City. This was the same gent who had come over to the office earlier, suggesting it wasn't an axle they had been working on the night before. What in blazes was he up to, anyway, sniffing around like that, then warning them about that supposed trio he had spotted in the saloon?

It was a cinch he had figured out what they were up to with this gold shipment, but just how much did he know? And damn it, wasn't this move of theirs supposed to be so slick no one would have guessed what they were up to? If this tall gent with the gunmetal blue eyes had been able to figure things out so easily, how many others had?

He didn't like it. No. He didn't like it, not one bit.

Beside him, Jed glanced over. "What's the matter, Mac? You ain't said a word since we left Rimrock."

"Ain't had nothin' to say."

"Yer face is all screwed up. I know the way it looks when yer tryin' to think. Ain't somethin' you do all that easy."

"Watch it, Jed," Mac said, smiling in spite of himself. "I might send you flyin' off this box and you'll have to walk home."

"Not on this trip, you won't." Jed chuckled. "You're stuck with me and you know it."

Mac turned his head to look full at Jed. The boy was pale, adenoidal, and he cut his hair with a hunting knife. He scratched a lot and picked his nose. And Mac had never seen him shoot the Greener, since he preferred not to have his worse fears justified. If the truth be told, Mac liked the kid well enough, but he had little faith in his ability as a shotgun.

"Yeah," he replied. "You're right. I'm stuck with you. I don't have no choice."

"Hey, Mac, c'mon. I was just kiddin'."

"I don't want your jokes, kid. I want you to keep that Greener ready."

"Jesus, Mac. You really expectin' trouble?"

"Now why in hell do you think Wells Fargo's got you ridin' shotgun messenger? So you can polish your ass on that seat?"

"Simmer down, Mac. Simmer down. No need to get riled."

Jed lapsed into hurt silence. Even if Mac was only half kidding, it was clear he was worried. He never would've lit into him like that if he wasn't worried for sure. But what in tarnation was Mac worried about? Who knew about this gold shipment beside them? Hell, he hadn't heard about the gold himself until a few minutes before pulling out of Rimrock.

Mac knew he had just hurt the kid's feelings. But it didn't bother him much, not if it made Jed take his job a little more seriously. He looked down at the glistening backs of the handsome Percheron brutes brought in specially to Rimrock for this run. So far they were working out just fine, but the true test of their stamina would be the steep grades they would have to negotiate when they reached the badlands.

• • •

Longarm felt the coach slowing as it approached a steep grade and roused himself from his doze. He heard the driver cracking his whip and bellowing at the horses, doing all he could to galvanize the beasts. He sat up, surprised that he had been able to sleep.

Mary Lou was peering intently out the window. After a moment she looked away from the towering rock faces enclosing the road and glanced at Longarm. Smiling abruptly, she leaned close to him.

"You got the time, mister?" Her eyes flicked to Longarm's pocket watch.

Longarm reached for it automatically.

With the speed of a striking rattler, the girl snatched the watch out of Longarm's grasp. With it came the chain and derringer. Longarm made a halfhearted attempt to snatch the derringer back, but she was too quick for him. Longarm found himself staring into her Colt's unblinking bore.

With a chuckle, the big man beside her reached over and lifted Longarm's .44 from his cross-draw rig.

"Now just settle back, Mr. Pinkerton," Mary Lou said. "You're gonna be raped, so you might as well enjoy it."

Chapter 4

The sun had shifted. The boulder beside which Carl Sutter crouched no longer protected him from the direct rays of the sun. Heavy beads of perspiration rolled down his face. Every once in a while he pulled out a filthy polka-dot handkerchief and mopped his brow. The back of his shirt was dark and rivulets of sweat trickled down the small of his back.

But Sutter was not thinking about the heat. He had more important considerations in mind at the moment. Such as them newly minted gold coins on that stage. And what he was going to do with them once they got their hands on them. Mary Lou and he had just about decided they would buy a horse ranch in California with their share. Dodger was mumbling about heading back East to open a saloon in Boston. Sutter did not care what he did, so long as he disappeared. He was getting damn sick of the fat bastard, and so was Mary Lou.

Sutter had chosen his spot carefully. Deep inside the badlands, this portion of the stage's route cut through a boulder-strewn landscape of towering rock and mesas. Crouched on a flat rock above the road, he had a clear, unobstructed view in both directions. By the time the stage reached the top of the grade, it would be almost directly beneath him. And with that enormous load the horses were hauling, the coach would be barely moving no matter how fiercely the driver lashed on the horses.

Sutter's Winchester rested on the boulder in front of him. He could smell the machine oil he had used to clean it baking in the sun. As he took out his handkerchief again to mop his forehead, he thought he heard the faint jingle of a harness. A second later he was sure of it and stood up to peer down the road. From behind the shielding walls of rock a cloud of dust lifted into the sky. The dim rumble of the coach's wheels came to him.

He jumped back down beside the boulder and snatched up his Winchester. Damn! It was almost hot enough to detonate the cartridges in the firing chamber. He flipped off the safety. The breech's searing metal stung his palm, but he paid no attention when he saw the stagecoach swing into view behind a massive boulder and start up the grade.

The stage driver was on his feet by this time, his whip snaking out over the backs of the powerful, straining brutes, its tip cracking again and again, echoing as sharply as gunshots among the rocks. Even so, the horses had to strain mightily to keep the stage moving as they lifted to the crest.

Sutter raised his Winchester. Curling his finger carefully, caressingly, around the trigger, he tucked the stock into the hollow of his shoulder and tracked the shotgun messenger. For a moment the sight rested on the young kid's hat brim, then shifted down to his leather vest. When the stage gained the crest, Sutter squeezed the trigger. The rifle's crack echoed off the rocks. The shotgun messenger flung up both hands and pitched sideways off the coach, his Greener dropping out of sight.

The stage driver sawed back on the ribbons. The horses reared in their traces as the stage came to a sudden rattling halt. Flinging down the reins, he reached for his own shotgun and stood up in the box, his eyes searching the towering rock walls on both sides of him.

Sutter stepped out from beside the boulder. "Drop that shotgun, mister! You won't be needin' it!"

The driver's face was scarlet with fury. "You murderin' son of a bitch! You shot Danny! You didn't give him a chance!"

"I'm givin' you a chance now, mister. But it's the only chance I'm going to give you. Drop that Greener!"

The driver hesitated. Smiling, Sutter swung up his rifle again. The driver cursed and flung his shotgun to the road. Sutter lowered his rifle and started to scramble down the shale-littered slope to the roadway.

Longarm was the first one out of the stage. Sally Henderson came after him with Mary Lou following, her Colt covering them both. In her tiny fist, it looked like a cannon. His own six-gun drawn, Dodger followed out after them like a cork popping out of a bottle.

Once clear of the stage, Longarm turned back around to face the coach. Sally Henderson, her face tight with fear and outrage, kept close beside him. Longarm was inwardly seething—not only at these outlaws, but at his own ineptitude. He had seen this coming a mile off. Yet, incredibly, he had let that grimy little whore disarm him as easily as if she were slicing a chocolate cake.

Sally Henderson's fingers dug into his arm. "Over there!" she cried, pointing. "Look!"

She was pointing at the sprawled figure lying face-down in a dark puddle of his own blood. It was the young shotgun messenger. Longarm had heard the outraged stage driver accusing the rifleman responsible—more than likely Carl Sutter—soon after he had brought the stage to a halt.

"There's nothing you can do," Longarm told her. "He's a dead man, looks like."

"But you can't be sure!"

When she started to run to the fallen man's side, Dodger planted his huge bulk in her path.

"Now, you just stay right where you are, Miss Pretty Pants," he told her. "You can't help that feller none. He's a gone beaver."

"But he may still be alive."

"Hell, you heard what your friend here said. He's already a dead man. Sutter can shoot the balls off a mosquito."

Mary Lou told Dodger to keep Longarm and Sally covered, then strode to the front of the stagecoach and glared up at the driver. "Throw down that strongbox, mister!"

The driver looked down for a long, miserable moment at this hard-faced slip of a girl, then threw down the steel strongbox. It slammed to the ground inches from Mary Lou's feet. Unfazed, she waggled her gun at him.

"All right. Now it's your turn. Get down here!"

Cursing, the driver dropped to the road, brushed insolently past her and hurried to the side of the shotgun messenger as Longarm caught sight of Carl Sutter picking his way swiftly toward them over a loose patch of shale.

Pulling up beside Mary Lou, he examined the strongbox, then shattered the padlock with a single bullet from his six-gun. He stepped back as Mary Lou flung open the lid and pulled forth the sacks of newly minted coins. With a squeal of delight, she held them up for Sutter to see.

Leaving Longarm and Sally Henderson, Dodger hustled over, crying, "Hey, don't forget my share!"

"We ain't divvying up now, Dodger. Besides, this here's just the frosting on the cake."

Sutter walked closer to the stage and reached in through the open door. Longarm heard him rapping smartly on the false floor with his revolver. Grinning, Sutter looked back at his two cohorts. "The floor's hollow, all right. The gold's in there, just like I said it would be."

The stage driver was on his feet suddenly. He turned and caught sight of Sutter. Without warning, he charged the man. "He's dead!" the distraught man cried. "You killed him! You killed Danny! You son of a bitch, he's dead!"

Sutter smiled. "So are you, asshole!"

Sutter flung up his Winchester, levered and fired from his hip. The side of the driver's head exploded. Blood spurted from it like catsup from a shattered bottle. Mac spun about, staggered a few steps, then sagged forward onto the ground. Sutter walked over to the stage driver. Despite the gaping wound in the side of his head, the man was still alive, slowly writhing in the bloody dust. Sally Henderson, weeping uncontrollably, turned away, burying her face in Longarm's chest. Sutter fired down into the stage driver's body. A tiny puff of dust exploded where the bullet entered.

Sutter turned to Dodger. "Get my horse."

"Where is it?"

"Down the road there. In among those rocks. Hurry it up. We got a long ways to go yet."

As Dodger hurried off, Sutter and Mary Lou turned their attention to Longarm and Sally Henderson. Approaching Longarm, Sutter was smiling again, a man happy in his work.

"Mary Lou just told me about you, mister. She had you pegged from the start. You're a Pinkerton." He chuckled. "She showed me that cute little derringer she took off you. Some watch fob."

"Not only that, but the watch keeps perfect time."

Stepping closer, Mary Lou reached into Longarm's inside breast pocket and deftly withdrew his wallet. When she opened it and saw the badge, she showed it to Sutter.

"Well, well," Sutter said. "So you ain't a Pinkerton. You're a U.S. deputy marshal." He shrugged. "Makes no difference. Anyone plant a hot slug in your gut, you all make the same sounds."

Reaching out, he grabbed Sally's wrist and flung her at Mary Lou. "Here. Take her."

"Why?" Mary Lou demanded.

"She's goin' with us."

"Who says so?"

"I do. Didn't you tell me Dodger's been sniffin' around?" When she nodded, he grinned. "Well, then, we'll just feed him Miss Pretty Pants here. That should keep him off your ass for a while."

Hearing these words and not mistaking their implications, Sally tried desperately to pull herself out of Mary Lou's grasp. Mary Lou yanked her close. Beside herself, Sally kicked out, catching Mary Lou in her right shin. She slapped Sally hard, then thrust her six-gun's barrel deep into Sally's stomach. Sally gasped for air.

Mary Lou withdrew her Colt's muzzle from Sally's midsection. Coughing dryly as she continued to gasp for air, Sally staggered back, the fight drained out of her.

"You silly little ass!" Mary Lou told her. "You can stay here if you want and feed the buzzards. Or you can come with us. That's all the choice you got."

Sally glanced pleadingly over at Longarm, as if he had the power to awaken her from this nightmare.

"Go with them, Sally," he told her. "I'm sorry. There's nothing I can do."

Longarm looked away from the despair in her face, hating himself for having to tell her what he did. But it was better for her to resign herself to the usages of this outlaw trio. At least for now. If she continued to fight them she'd end up with those two dead men sprawled in the road, just as Mary Lou promised.

Dodger rode up on Sutter's horse, swung off it, and lumbered toward them. The first thing he noticed was Mary Lou hanging onto a sullen Sally Henderson.

"What're you doin' with her, Mary Lou?"

"Surprise. Carl says we're taking her with us. Now you can keep your grubby hands off me."

"Mary Lou, you know I never tried nothing with you."

"Maybe *you* didn't, but your hands sure been busy."

Dodger looked unhappily at Sutter. "Jesus, Carl. She's exaggerating."

"Prove it."

"How?"

"Kill this bastard here. He ain't no Pinkerton. We just found out he's a U.S. deputy marshal."

"You want *me* to kill him?"

"Ain't you up to it?"

"It ain't that," the fat man said, shifting uncomfortably under Sutter's harsh glare. "It's just that he ain't comin' at me or nothing."

"Oh, shit," Mary Lou said, reaching back for her Colt, "if Dodger ain't up to it, I'll take care of the marshal myself."

"No, no," Dodger said hastily, drawing his own weapon. "I'll do it. I can finish this bastard off."

"Do it then," Sutter told him, grabbing his horse's reins and starting for the coach. "And hurry it up. It won't take us long to load that strongbox in the coach." He glanced at Mary Lou. "Let's go."

As Mary Lou hurried after Sutter, dragging Sally with her, Sally looked back at Longarm in pure dismay. She seemed dazed, as if she could not believe that this was really happening to her.

But Longarm had no doubt. This was for real. For the Dodger, too—as Longarm now thought of him. Robbing a stage was one thing. But cold-blooded murder was something else again. The Dodger now found himself out of his depth. He mopped his brow nervously.

"Nervous?" Longarm asked.

"Hell, no," he lied. "I ain't nervous."

"Wouldn't blame you if you were. Killin' a man in cold blood ain't all that easy."

"You don't think so?"

"I know so."

"I'll get used to it."

"If you hang with them two over there much longer, you'll have to get used to it."

"Why shouldn't I stay with them?"

The Dodger seemed to want to continue this crazy discussion—anything to delay the moment when he'd have to pull the trigger on Longarm.

"No reason, I guess. If you're sure Sutter won't deal you out when the time comes to divvy up the spoils."

"Sutter wouldn't do that."

"Not if you do what he says."

"That's right."

"So you better get on with it, Dodger."

The Dodger raised the revolver. "Yeah."

"You going to do it here—right out in the middle of the road?"

"Sure."

"Why not over there near the rocks? There's more shade."

"Jesus Christ, what the hell difference would that make?"

"I'm thinking you might miss something vital. If you do, I'll be lying in that hot sun, waiting for the vultures to pick me apart."

"I'll aim for your head. You won't feel a thing."

"Well, that's right decent of you, Dodger. But it sure don't give me no comfort, considering your handicap."

"What handicap?"

"Your hog fat. The way I see it, you can hardly get out of your own way, let alone fire that cannon accurately."

The Dodger's tiny eyes blazed with sudden fury.

45

Longarm could almost read his mind. The man was thinking that Longarm was like all the others, toying with him, making a fool of him. The Dodger thumb-cocked his Colt with sudden resolve. But Longarm had been inching closer to the Dodger. He flung himself at the man, his left hand closing about his Colt's barrel. He twisted violently.

The Colt detonated harmlessly and with a sudden squeal of pain, the Dodger dropped the gun. Longarm flung himself at the man, grappling with him in an effort to get to the ground. But Longarm found the Dodger's bulk as intimidating as his stench. Grunting with exertion, he remained on his feet and punched crazily at Longarm with all the fury of a drunken man. Longarm fended off the wild flurry, burrowed in, and managed to catch the Dodger on the chin, rocking him back. But when he followed this up with another punch to the fat man's head, it only seemed to jar the Dodger into renewed ferocity.

Like an enraged grizzly, he charged through Longarm's punches and, clasping his hands into a single giant fist, pounded Longarm on his right shoulder, nearly driving him into the ground. Longarm's knees sagged. He shook his head and flung a desperate roundhouse at the Dodger, who paid no attention as he pounded Longarm repeatedly on the head. Longarm's hat went flying. The ground slammed him in the back. Dazedly, he stared up at the Dodger. The fat man had swept up his Colt and was aiming it down at Longarm.

But when the detonation came, it was from a distant rifle, high in the rocks.

Clutching at his forearm, the Dodger dropped his gun as he glanced frantically up at the rocks. Then he spun about to look over at the coach. Mary Lou had been running over to help Dodger, but had already turned and was racing back to the stagecoach.

"Sutter! I been hit!" the Dodger squealed. "There's someone in the rocks!"

Wonderfully revived, Longarm scrambled for the fat man's dropped Colt. Before he could get to it, though, the Dodger kicked the gun away. Longarm grabbed his ankle and tried to pull the man down.

"Dodger!" Sutter cried. "Come on! Leave the bastard!"

Sutter was in the act of tying his horse to the rear of the coach. A second shot cracked from above. Leaving the horse, he vaulted up into the coach's box and snatched up the ribbons. A third round whined off the baggage rack behind him.

Hastily kicking himself free of Longarm's grasp, the Dodger raced for the stagecoach. It was already moving. Sutter's whip slashed at the straining horses. Mary Lou opened the door. The staggering Dodger flung his bulk into the stage. As Mary Lou hauled him in and closed the door, another shot came from above. This round took a chunk out of the door.

The stagecoach gained speed rapidly and in a moment had rocked out of sight.

Chapter 5

The man Longarm saw leading his horse down the steep slope toward him had a star pinned to his vest. Longarm guessed him to be close to fifty. He had a walrus mustache and a thick white shock of hair that hung clear to his shoulders. As he neared Longarm, his blue eyes had the keenness of a knife blade. Broad shouldered, he moved with the sure, easy grace of a healthy animal.

Longarm didn't think he would need to be introduced. This had to be Sheriff Tom Billings on his way back to Rimrock.

"Looks like you saved my ass, Sheriff."

"That's the way it looks."

He kept on past Longarm to inspect the two sprawled bodies. Longarm followed him. The sheriff gazed down at the stagecoach driver for a long moment, his face dark, then moved on to the shotgun messenger. This time he took a deep breath and spun angrily to face Longarm.

"I warned that fool."

"What fool?"

"The Wells Fargo manager in Rimrock."

"You mean you knew of his plan to hide the gold shipment under a false bottom on the stagecoach?"

"Looks like you did, too."

"That's right. I did."

"Well, don't take any credit for it. Everyone this side of St. Louis heard about that crazy scheme of his. That's why I tried to talk him out of it."

"Too bad you weren't successful."

Billings turned his sharp eyes on Longarm. "You got a name, mister?"

"Name's Long. Custis Long."

Billings shook Longarm's hand. The grip was powerful. "Tom Billings. I'm the sheriff at Rimrock." He gazed off after the coach. "How many outlaws were there?"

"Three. One was a girl, the toughest of the lot, I'd say."

"I recognized the one drove off the stage. A real hard case. Been hanging around Rimrock for a week."

"They took a passenger with them. A woman, Sally Henderson. She's from the East, on her way out to Mountain City to teach school."

Billings blew out his cheeks and tore off his hat. "Damn. Looks like she's goin' to get a few lessons herself." He glanced down the road at the horse Sutter had left behind. It was peacefully cropping a patch of grass in among some rocks. "Can you ride, Long?"

"I think I'll be able to stay in the saddle, Sheriff."

"Well, there's your mount over there then. Ride back to Rimrock and send out my deputy. I'm going after them bastards."

"If you're going after Sutter, I'm going with you."

"You sure you're up to it, Long?"

"I'm up to it."

"You didn't look like it wrestling with that fat slob."

Billings strode over to his horse. Stepping quickly into his saddle, he gathered up his reins and looked coldly down at Longarm. "What are you waiting for, mister? Haul ass. We ain't got all day."

Longarm almost saluted as he hustled past the mounted sheriff on his way to the horse. As he went, he stooped quickly, snatched up the Colt left by the Dodger and dropped it into his cross-draw rig.

Huddled inside the coach, Sally glared at the two sitting across from her. The fat man was clutching his wounded right arm, a look of pure agony on his face. His blood darkened his entire right sleeve and the front of his vest. Through the tightly clasped fingers of his left hand, the blood was oozing steadily.

The demoralizing fear that had paralyzed her earlier had given way to a monumental, all-consuming fury. Because of these outlaws, these filthy barbarians sitting across from her, two good men were dead. And it was only through some miraculous intervention that Custis remained alive. She had no idea who the rifleman was who had shot the fat man, but had it been a lightning bolt from God Almighty Himself, she could not have been more pleased.

51

The fat man was whimpering like a child, incapable of accepting his pain with any show of manly forbearance. He disgusted her utterly. The bullet appeared to have entered his right arm just below the shoulder. When he saw her looking at him, he stopped moaning and glared balefully back at her, as if in some crazy way she was the one responsible for his agony.

"What're you lookin' at?" Dodger growled.

"I am looking at a swine," she replied boldly. "A miserable, contemptible specimen of humanity. That wound you have sustained only serves you right."

The girl looked at the fat man, a wry smile on her face. "Hey, Dodger, you going to let your girl friend talk to you like that?"

"Hell, no," he said, grinning.

He leaned over and slapped Sally with his left hand. The force of it caused her teeth to slash the tip of her tongue. She felt the warm blood welling in her mouth. Her senses reeling, she leaned back and wiped her mouth with the back of her hand. When she saw the blood, she looked back at the fat man with pure loathing.

"You're lucky I don't pitch you out of this coach, you bitch," Dodger told her. "The next time you show your temper, I will."

His words appalled her as much as did his brutal slap. She resolved quickly to restrain her outrage. She was not dealing with normal human beings. These were creatures from another world. Looking away from them, she glanced out the window. They had left the road to Mountain City some distance back and were now careening along a narrow, twisting trail through a land of towering rocks and steep-sided, winding gullies, a rough terrain that seemed to be taking a great deal out of the stage. How it managed to stay in one piece she could not understand. And the horses were being used mercilessly, judging from the way Sutter shouted and lashed at them. His fury alone, it seemed, was what kept the poor brutes plunging recklessly on through this treacherous land.

Abruptly, she became aware of Sutter hauling back on the reins. The brake shoes squealed and the skidding wheels sent gravel flying as the stage rattled to a halt. The stage rocked as Sutter jumped down.

He pulled open the door and leaned in. "Get out of here," he told them. "We got work to do."

Dodger, protesting the pain as he clutched his wounded arm, eased himself from his seat and stumbled out of the coach. Mary Lou waved Sally out ahead of her. Sally stepped out into the blazing sunshine, brushed past Sutter and a short distance from the stage sat down in the shade of a boulder. Sutter had halted on the crest of the trail they had been following. There was a sheer rock wall at the foot of the trail, and on the right of it a steep ravine. She had never known such wild country; no matter in which direction she looked, there was not a single stone or blade of grass that had ever known the touch of a human hand.

Sutter approached Dodger. The fat man was still on his feet, leaning back against the stagecoach, his face a doughy white from loss of blood.

"How bad you hit, Dodger?"

"I'll live, Carl."

"Well, you know what we got to do. That son of a bitch who shot you might be on our tail right now, and we got to transfer the gold to packhorses. You think you can pull your weight?"

"I'll help, damn it. Just give me a chance to stop this bleeding."

"Here. Let me see." Sutter's inspection of the damaged arm was cursory. Stepping back, he looked at Dodger and shook his head. "Shit! The bone ain't broke. The bullet went clear through."

"Yeah, but I'm bleedin' like a stuck pig."

"Well, damn it, stop the bleeding and lend a hand. We ain't got no time for a cripple."

Whining all the while, Dodger managed to fashion a crude tourniquet with his bandanna, then joined Sutter and Mary Lou as they backed the horses out of their traces and over to the side of the trail. There, behind boulders shielded by a tangle of scrub pine, Sutter had cached saddles and other gear. They saddled three of the Percherons for riding, then fitted leather aparejos on the others. The three outlaws led the horses over to the stagecoach. Sutter clambered into the coach and tried to pry up the floorboards with a shovel blade. The task went depressingly slow, however, and after a particularly violent wrench by the impatient Sutter, the blade snapped.

In a fury of frustration, Sutter flung the broken implement from the coach and climbed out. Moaning softly, Dodger collapsed wearily in the shade of a stunted pine. His wound was bleeding again, and he seemed unwilling or unable to do anything to staunch the flow. Obviously frustrated, Sutter stood beside Mary Lou and surveyed the stagecoach balefully. Things were not going according to plan.

"You should have brought a wrecking bar," Mary Lou told Sutter.

"I know."

"So what the hell are we going to do now?"

He walked away from her and peered down the trail at the canyon wall below the crest. Then he came back. "I got an idea," he told her.

"It sure as hell better be a good one."

"We'll push the stagecoach down this grade," Sutter told her. "It'll be going at a good speed and smash to pieces when it hits that canyon wall. Then we'll pick it clean."

Mary Lou glanced down the trail at the canyon wall. "Might work," she admitted. "But then I don't see we got much choice."

Sutter looked over at Dodger. "Get over here," he told him. Then he looked at Sally. "You too, Pretty Pants."

Sally got up slowly, unwilling to do anything that might help these outlaws. Seeing her reluctance, Sutter snarled at her to hurry the hell up. Sally decided she had no choice and walked over to lend her back to the effort.

The coach had come to rest close to the crest of the trail and Sally saw at once what they intended. But nudging the gold-laden coach the few feet it would take to get it beyond the crest proved to be a difficult task. The four of them strained mightily and were just barely able to get the wheels turning. It was with considerable relief that Sally straightened up finally and watched the coach rumble down the trail under its own momentum.

Groaning and lurching like something alive, the coach rapidly picked up speed as it headed directly for the canyon wall. It promised to be a terrific crash. Sutter and Mary Lou trotted down the trail after it. But halfway down the trail, the coach's right front wheel struck a boulder embedded in the trail. The coach leaped crazily, then veered wildly to the right, struck another boulder, and lunged into the air. It came down so hard it lost a wheel, tipped wildly and began to cartwheel into the ravine beside the trail, shedding parts of itself as it vanished from sight.

Sally hung back as Mary Lou and Sutter clambered down into the ravine after the coach. When Sally reached the edge of the ravine, she peered down and saw Mary Lou and Sutter poking through the wreckage. When Sutter and Mary Lou climbed wearily back up onto the trail, Sutter yelled to Dodger, beckoning impatiently to him. Dodger took his time, and when he reached them, it was obvious the man was not going to be much help.

"I don't know if I can do much, Carl," Dodger whined. "I'm as weak as a kitten."

"Some kitten," said Mary Lou.

"Hell, Dodger," Sutter told him, "the stage floor is all busted up. All we got to do now is load the horses."

Dodger peered uneasily down the ravine's steep slope. "Shit, Carl. I can't go down there. Why don't you let me go back and get the horses."

"No. I'm sending Mary Lou for them. And you're going down there on your feet or headfirst. It's your choice."

"All right, Carl," Dodger groaned wearily. "All right. Ain't no need for you to talk like that."

Sutter glanced over at Sally. "You, too, Pretty Pants. You're going down there too. Time you earned your keep."

Sally saw no sense in protesting, not when she saw the look in Sutter's eyes.

As Mary Lou hurried off to get the horses, Sally followed the two men down the slope. It was frighteningly steep, the ground underfoot treacherous. Deep gullies were filled with shifting gravel; at the lightest brush, loose chunks of soil went tumbling down the slope ahead of her. When she grabbed roots or shrubs to hang on to, they pulled free. Twice she sprawled forward onto her hands and knees, reaching out fruitlessly each time for something to grab. Not once did the men below glance back to see how she was doing, ignoring completely her muffled cries. By the time she reached the bottom of the ravine, her arms and elbows were raw, her shins skinned, and her skirt torn in several places. She had lost her straw boater in the first few minutes of her descent.

The stagecoach was a sad, broken shambles. Three of its wheels had spun off into the brush. The floor of the coach had impaled itself onto a powerful ridged boulder, which had burst up through it, sending the pouches of gold coins exploding into the air. Scattered all around the wreckage, like treasure spilling forth from the vaults of King Midas, were the freshly minted gold coins that had burst out of the pouches.

Wasting no time, Sutter and the fat man began gathering up what pouches were still intact. Watching them contemptuously, Sally leaned back wearily against a boulder. So caught up were the two men by the sight of all this gleaming wealth, they paid no attention to her until Sutter finished picking up the intact leather pouches and glancing up, saw her standing in front of the boulder.

"What the hell are you doing, Pretty Pants?" he demanded angrily. "Get over here and help out!" He tossed some empty pouches at her. "Gather up the gold on the ground and fill these pouches."

Sally set to work. Despite her lack of enthusiasm for the task, she had gathered up quite a fortune by the time Mary Lou plunged down the slope.

Emerging from the coach, Sutter asked her, "Where's the horses?"

"They're on the trail right above us."

"What the hell're they doing up there? It'll take us forever to lug this gold up that slope. It's too heavy. We need to load them packhorses down here."

"You mean bring the horses down that slope? You must be crazy."

"I ain't crazy. There's a break in the ravine a quarter mile down. Take the horses down that way, and lead them back here."

"I'll need help."

"Take Pretty Pants."

Mary Lou looked balefully at Sally. "Follow me."

Sally straightened up, brushed a damp patch of hair out of her eyes and followed Mary Lou back up the slope.

Longarm and Sheriff Tom Billings found no difficulty following the coach's tracks when it turned off the Mountain City road onto the narrow trail. Once they reached the trail's crest where the coach had been sent careening, they dismounted, followed the coach's tracks on foot and found themselves peering down into the ravine at the shattered stagecoach below—and the four people moving purposefully about it.

The two men led their horses back off the trail and tied them up, then worked themselves carefully down the steep slope. Longarm had only the Colt, while the sheriff carried a Winchester and a Colt. When they got close enough to see the four clearly, the sheriff halted Longarm to study the situation.

Four of the stage's horses had been saddled, while three were being used as packhorses. Sally Henderson was being forced to load the gold onto the aparejos. She worked with precious little urgency, Longarm noted. But Sutter and Mary Lou—and to some extent, the wounded fat man—were making up for her lack of enthusiasm as they rapidly loaded the gold onto the pack-horses.

"Go around behind them," the sheriff told Longarm. "Stay in that patch of scrub pine when you cross over. You'll come out in those rocks. I'll wait until I see you disappear into them."

"Then what?"

"When I see you're in position, I'll fire a warning shot and tell them they're surrounded."

"Suppose they go for their weapons?"

"If they do, I'll take Sutter out first. If they make a run for it, you'll get a clear shot from those rocks."

"Aren't you forgetting something?"

"What?"

"Sally Henderson."

"Hell, Long. I won't be aiming at her. Besides, she'll probably break for cover as soon as I open up."

"If she gets the chance, you mean."

Billings frowned as he digested that. "You're right, damn it. They could grab her first thing. They wouldn't hesitate to use her as a shield."

"That's what I was thinking."

"But hell, Long. We can't just open up on them without a warning."

"I wasn't suggesting that."

Billings looked at him. In his manner now Longarm thought he caught a grudging awareness that perhaps Longarm was not completely incompetent. "All right, mister. What's your suggestion?"

"When I reach the rocks, I'll get Sally's attention, beckon to her to sneak away. Soon as she's safe with me, I'll fire a single shot into the air. When you answer my fire, they'll know they're surrounded."

"You think you can get her attention?"

"All I can do is try. If you've got a better idea, let's hear it."

"We'll give it a try then. I'll wait for your shot."

Making it across to the other side of the ravine was not easy. Debris from too many centuries past littered the ground. Boulders of all sizes and shapes lay everywhere, like the discarded building blocks of some titanic architect. A tangle of scrub pine and brush grew with dense luxuriance between the boulders. Windfalls and trees that had been washed off the slopes lay everywhere and wild grape vines made for a devilish tangle. Not until he reached the gravelly streambed in the center of the ravine did the going get any easier. And during all this, he could not allow himself to make a sound.

Reaching the rocks finally, he moved into them until the shattered stagecoach was between him and the outlaws. Then, clambering higher into them, he chose a site that gave him an unobstructed view of the stagecoach and the outlaws beyond toiling feverishly beyond it. They had just about finished loading up the packhorses. Sally Henderson had turned away from a loaded packhorse and was now slumped wearily against a tree.

"Look up here!" Longarm muttered. "Up here, damn it!"

But Sally's head was bowed in weariness, her face turned away from Longarm. The fat man, holding onto his wounded arm, seemed to be getting all the attention. He had slumped down on a boulder and seemed unable or unwilling to get up as Mary Lou and Sutter huddled around him, obviously doing what they could to goad him back onto his feet.

This was his only chance to catch Sally's attention. He moved swiftly back down the rocks and darted across the streambed, crouched behind the stagecoach wreckage, and waited for Sally to look in his direction. Meanwhile, Longarm could hear Mary Lou and Sutter clearly as they urged the Dodger to get up and ride out with them. But the fat man seemed unwilling to move, his whining protestations echoing in the narrow gorge. Suddenly, inexplicably, Sally Henderson turned her face in Longarm's direction and the two found themselves looking into each other's eyes.

Before Longarm could put his finger to his mouth to keep her silent, she cried out and darted toward him. Longarm groaned as Sutter whirled and overtook Sally in two quick strides. Flinging her around, he punched her in the face. As she hit the ground he left her, drew his Colt and moved cautiously in Longarm's direction. He could not see Longarm, who had ducked low as soon as Sally cried out, and who waited now for Sutter to get close enough for a clear shot. With Sutter out of it, Longarm hoped the other two would be demoralized enough to throw up their hands. Abruptly, realizing his vulnerability, Sutter held up, then moved quickly back to where he had flung Sally to the ground.

Pulling her roughly to her feet, he faced the rocks behind Longarm and cried, "Whoever is out there, you better not try anything. You do, and I'll kill this woman! I warn you! We are desperate men!"

Keeping his rifle down, Longarm gave no response.

"Give me my rifle," Sutter told Mary Lou.

She tossed it to him.

Levering quickly, he sent three rounds into the rocks behind Longarm, the bullets ricocheting loudly in the ravine's narrow confines. Lifting his head slightly, Longarm glimpsed Sutter holding a terrified Sally Henderson at his side as he peered across the streambed, searching for sign of the man Sally had tried to join.

At the moment, Longarm realized, with Sally as their hostage, the three outlaws held all the cards. Ducking low, he moved off down the streambed until he was able to cross undetected back into the rocks. Once he was safe among them, Billings punched a shot into the air.

"This is Sheriff Billings," he cried. "You ain't goin' nowhere, Sutter. We got you surrounded!"

To bolster the sheriff's threat, Longarm sent a shot into the air.

"Maybe you got us surrounded," the defiant Sutter yelled back, "but we got the girl. Follow us too close and we'll finish her off."

There was no doubt Sutter would carry out his threat. Longarm watched in miserable frustration as Sutter mounted up, then flung Sally Henderson over the horse's neck. One hand held the reins, the other his Colt, the muzzle resting on Sally's neck. Mary Lou and the Dodger mounted up quickly, and leading their gold-laden packhorses, the three outlaws rode out into the streambed.

Seething in frustration, Longarm stood up and watched them ride out of sight.

Chapter 6

Jenny Wills had long since taken the reins back from Josh and they were almost through the badlands when he stood up on the seat and pointed.

"Look, Ma," he cried eagerly. "There's Lone Bear!"

Jenny quickly pulled the boy back down and glanced in the direction Josh had indicated. An Indian astride his pony stood out clearly against the sky on a bluff overlooking the trail. His powerful, blocky figure, topped off by a single feather in his headband, was pleasantly familiar to Jenny, as well as to Josh and Annie. Jenny halted the team and waved. Lone Bear waved back and vanished from the bluff. With the wagon halted, Annie stirred to life and squinted confusedly about her, obviously wondering why they had stopped since they had not yet arrived at the ranch. Josh put his arm around her. Annie snuggled against her brother and promptly went back to sleep. Jenny flipped the reins and started up again.

A quarter of a mile farther on, the Indian rode out from behind a clump of pine and headed toward them. When he reached the wagon, Jenny slowed the horses to a walk and greeted him with a smile. Turning his horse the Indian kept pace with the wagon in a casual escort.

Lone Bear was a Cimarron, or Southern Ute. His chief had been the great Ignacio. Though he was not a member of the northern Ute bands, which had participated in the battle of Red Canyon, Lone Bear and other members of his band had not obeyed the horse soldiers and gone south with the rest of the Ute. They had remained in the area—hidden, invisible, ghosts on horseback—haunting the badlands adjoining Jenny's ranch.

But Jenny would be the last person to tell anyone in Rimrock that Lone Bear and a few of his tribesmen still hunted in the vicinity of her ranch. For the past two winters it had been Lone Bear and other members of his band who had watched over Jenny and her children like hawks, twice scaring off Apaches fleeing from Crook.

"What are you doing here, Lone Bear?" Jenny asked.

"I wait for you," he replied.

Jenny smiled, amused as always at Lone Bear's inability or unwillingness to mask his motive with a casual lie. Any gentleman from the East would have doffed his hat, smiled, and said he just happened to be in the vicinity when he caught sight of her carriage in the distance. She flipped the reins once more to increase the team's pace, and a half hour later they broke from the badlands, and with Long Bear still alongside, rode out into the valley. A little later, they splashed across the stream that meandered in a broad, flat band beside her ranch house.

Breathing a sigh of relief, Jenny pulled up beside the barn. With Lone Bear's help, she unhitched the horses and led them into the barn while Josh slung the exhausted Annie over his little shoulder and carried her in to her bed. After she and Lone Bear took care of the horses and finished carrying the provisions into the house, Jenny made some fresh lemonade and brought it out onto the porch. Lone Bear who was sitting in his favorite wicker chair gratefully accepted a glass from Jenny. After pouring herself a glass, she slumped wearily in her favorite rocker beside Lone Bear.

"Now then, Lone Bear," she said, "what brings you so far from your people?"

He promptly pulled the Bible she had only recently given him from the leather pouch he had brought with him from the barn. He smiled quickly, his teeth brilliant in his dark, handsome face. "I have trouble with a passage in your people's Bible. I will find place. Will you help me?"

"Of course, Lone Bear."

Lone Bear's powerful fingers swiftly flipped the pages. Coming to the passage that bothered him, he read it aloud, his voice rumbling powerfully in his massive chest.

". . . And God spoke unto Noah, saying, Go forth from the ark, thou, and thy wife, and thy sons, and thy sons' wives with thee.

"Bring forth with thee every living thing that is with thee, of all flesh, both of fowl, and of cattle, and of every creeping thing that creepeth upon the earth; that they may breed abundantly in the earth, and be fruitful, and multiply upon the earth. . . ."

He halted and looked up from the page, a frown on his face. "I did not find this to be the speech of my white friends. It sounds strange to my ears. What does 'thee' and 'thou' mean?"

"It means 'you'," Jenny explained.

"Then why does the writer not use that word?"

"The King James version of the Bible was translated many, many years ago, Lone Bear. And that form of address was the appropriate style in those days."

Lone Bear accepted this explanation, but his frown remained. He closed the book and looked unhappily at Jenny.

"All that rain come down!" he said to her, his face registering eloquently the wonder of it.

"Yes, it *was* a great deal of rain, Lone Bear."

"For forty days and forty nights. But why did it not drown the insects that live under the rocks? Did Noah search out two of them also, along with two of the camel and two of the buffalo? And what of the worms that live in the ground, the scorpions that hide in the dark places? Did Noah find two of them also? I think there must be too many creatures under the ground and in the sea for that one old man to find. I think that ark must be a very big boat to hold so many creatures, bigger even than the riverboats I see one time on the Mississippi."

In spite of herself, Jenny smiled. "You might have a point there, Lone Bear. I have often wondered about that crowded ark myself."

Lone Bear seemed pleased that she not only understood his perplexity, but shared it as well. He seemed to relax then, and Jenny leaned back in her chair, grateful to be back at her ranch again—and to have Lone Bear sitting with her.

Two years before, when Lone Bear first entered the ranch house and caught sight of her late husband's modest library, he had been like a child in front of a Christmas tree. His eyes had lit up and he had promptly asked Jenny if he might borrow a book. Astonished, she asked if he could read, and he had explained that when he was a young brave, his tribe had found a nearly frozen missionary in a snow-clogged pass. The old man died the following spring, but before he passed on, he had managed to teach Lone Bear how to read.

She had let the Indian borrow a book, and it did not take long for her to discover that his appetite for the printed word was all but insatiable. He devoured every work of history, biography, and fiction in her library, then fell to reading even Jenny's almanacs and mail-order catalogues.

In order to discuss the books he had read and the ideas they generated, Jenny had found it necessary for her to read almost as widely as Lone Bear, with the result that over the intervening months she had become, in a sense, not only Lone Bear's teacher, but his pupil as well.

"Storm come," Lone Bear said, glancing up.

She followed his gaze and saw thunderheads building in the sky above the badlands. In the short time since they had unloaded the wagon, the air had grown heavy, even a bit sultry. She could feel the sudden damp chill as the storm approached and was grateful it had held off until they reached the ranch. In a cloudburst, the narrow trail she had followed through the badlands could have become a fearsome maelstrom.

"Lone Bear," she said, turning back to him, "was there anything else in the Bible you did not understand?"

The Indian nodded, his eyes glowing at once with the excitement that always came on him during these discussions. He leafed quickly through the Bible. Jenny was pleased to see how familiar he had become with it and how swiftly he was able to locate its various passages. When he found the one he wanted, he began to read the passage aloud to her. Leaning back in her rocker, Jenny listened intently. The passage dealt with the destruction of Sodom and Gomorrah. When Lone Bear had finished reading it, he looked quickly up at Jenny and asked how the Lord could have killed all those people, saving only Lot's family.

Jenny immediately felt out of her depth, but she could sense Lone Bear's genuine concern and was anxious to allay it. "The inhabitants of those two cities were very wicked," she explained. "They deserved to die. But Lot was a righteous man, so the Lord made an exception in his case."

Lone Bear leaned back in his chair, his eyes alight. "Ah!" he said. "These people who live in these cities, they were wicked, very wicked?"

"Oh, yes."

"Why? What did these people do?"

Jenny felt herself blushing. His blunt question had sent her again out of her depth. In truth, she had never been certain herself just what crimes the citizens of those two doomed cities had committed, though she was vaguely aware that it had to do with fornication and other acts of licentiousness, difficult for her to imagine and none of which she was anxious to discuss with Lone Bear.

"I only know they were wicked, Lone Bear. They . . . did things that were an abomination in the eyes of God. They displeased him and persisted in their evil ways."

Lone Bear nodded solemnly.

"I have seen such cities with my own eyes," he said, his voice heavy with disapproval. "One such is Mountain City. It is always the same when the white men come together to dig gold and silver from the ground. And when they come to build rails for the iron horse, they also make such cities. The women who come to these places are as bad as the men. They drink the firewater with them, and these women will have as many men as can pay them. I have seen it. Yes, your God must not like such places."

Jenny hoped Lone Bear did not notice how she was blushing, and nodded quickly. He had certainly got the gist of it. "Yes, Lone Bear. That's what Sodom and Gomorrah were like, I am sure."

"And that is why the Lord consumed them with his fire?"

"Yes," Jenny assured him.

"But was Lot's wife not a good woman?"

"Yes, of course she was."

Lone Bear frowned. "Then why did the Lord turn her into a pillar of salt?"

"Because she looked back at the cities while they were being destroyed," Jenny told him lamely. Her voice quivered slightly, since this passage concerning

71

Ruth was something she, personally, had never been able to abide.

"Is it such a sin then to look back and see the power of the Lord's destruction?" The Indian was obviously struggling to understand.

Jenny tried to explain. "The Lord told Lot that he was not to look back, and that no one in his family was to do so, either. When Lot's wife looked back, she disobeyed the Lord. So He punished her."

Lone Bear closed the Bible. "I think your Lord must be a cruel master," Lone Bear said with great sadness—and compassion. It was almost as if he had been looking for a friend in these pages and had failed to find one.

Anxious to end this unnerving discussion, but not willing to see Lone Bear's new faith shattered so easily, Jenny said, "Lone Bear, you must understand that the Lord is like a parent to his children."

"Is that so?"

"Yes. So you see, he must punish them if they disobey."

"I would not turn any of my children to salt if they disobeyed."

"You do not have any children," she reminded him sharply.

"That is true," the Indian admitted, his face falling. "I do not."

At once Jenny was sorry she had spoken so bluntly. Sometimes the acuity of Lone Bear's sensitivity amazed Jenny.

"You must forgive me, Lone Bear," she said gently. "I am still tired from my trip to Rimrock. Perhaps I spoke too sharply. I did not mean to do so. And sometimes," she admitted with a smile. "I myself do not

72

always understand the Bible or the ways of the Lord."

He relaxed and sat back in the wicker chair, obviously grateful for her comforting words.

"Lone Bear," she asked suddenly, "why don't you take a woman? I have seen some of the young girls of your people. They are very beautiful."

Lone Bear shrugged, his face remaining impassive. "These young women say Lone Bear's head is full of strange things, and his words are even more strange. They say he will never keep food in his woman's lodge or bring furs to keep her warm when it is winter. They say he is not a warrior because all he can do is read the white man's words. So now these women laugh when Lone Bear asks for them to come live in his lodge."

"That is too bad," Jenny said, genuinely concerned. "You must be very lonely."

"Lone Bear is not alone when he reads. He hears the voices speaking to him from the pages. And he is not alone when he comes to this lodge and talks of what he reads with Jenny Wills."

"I'm glad, Lone Bear," Jenny said.

She was reaching for her glass of lemonade when Josh appeared from around the corner of the ranch house. He was running full tilt.

"What's for supper, Ma?" he asked, charging up onto the porch. "I'm starved!"

"That's an exaggeration, Josh, and you know it."

Annie appeared in the doorway, rubbing the sleep out of her eyes. "I'm hungry too," she announced sleepily as she climbed almost blindly up into Jenny's lap.

Jenny laughed, and taking Annie's hand, got to her feet. Pausing as she started back into the house to get supper ready, she said, "Lone Bear, would you care to join us for supper?"

His teeth gleamed. "What will Jenny Wills have for dessert?"

"Apple cobbler," Jenny said at once, aware it was his favorite.

"Then Lone Bear will stay."

Getting to his feet, he put the Bible back in his leather pouch and looked at Josh. "Lone Bear will take this young warrior for ride on his pony. Maybe then he will not think only of his stomach."

Already accustomed to such rides, Josh agreed instantly. Lone Bear lifted Josh up onto his shoulders and strode off toward the barn.

Watching them go, Jenny suddenly frowned. An alarming thought had just occurred to her. Were Lone Bear's visits to her ranch solely for the purpose of discussing what he had read? And what about her? Why had she given him that Bible? Why had it become so important to her that he know about it—and through it the religion of her people? Was it because she was beginning to think of Lone Bear as more than just a friendly Indian?

As a possible suitor, perhaps?

The thought was too unnerving—frightening, even. She sat suddenly back down in her rocker, her heart pounding, and pulled Annie up onto her lap. What on earth was the matter with her? How could she possibly think of herself as Lone Bear's squaw?

A clap of thunder rattled the canyon's walls. Longarm glanced up. Dark, tumbling clouds were scudding in swiftly over the badlands. With them came a damp gust of wind, as if someone had opened a vast root cellar. Longarm snugged his hat down securely; heavy drops of rain splattered onto his head and shoulders. As the raindrops began thudding heavily down, he realized that if this rain kept up for any length of time, they would have no more wagon tracks to follow.

It did. And before long, the thunderstorm became a cloudburst. They kept on doggedly through the narrow canyon, bent before the lashing rain until the tracks they were following were swallowed up in a rapidly rising torrent that swept on past them. The horses' fetlocks were completely submerged by this time and it would not be long before the water reached their knees.

They decided it was high time they got the hell out of the canyon. Splashing ashore onto a stretch of caprock, they dismounted and led their horses up the canyon's steep flank. The driving rain turned the slope into a shifting quagmire, and they were lucky to find at last a reasonably dry spot under a overhanging rock shelf. It was, they judged, high enough to keep them out of the reach of the torrent building swiftly in the canyon below. Tying their horses to some tough old pines, they made a miserable camp close in among the rock face.

They made no effort to build a fire. The driving, wind-whipped rain made that an impossibility. Longarm leaned back against the rock wall and took out two cheroots. Handing one to Billings, he unwrapped his own and lit up.

Billings took the cheroot gratefully. "We ain't doin' so well," he admitted dryly, lighting up. "But I ain't worried none. We'll get them bastards."

"If you say so, Sheriff."

"I don't say so. I know so. This rain will delay us,

but it sure as hell won't stop us. No way. Besides, they must have had to go for higher ground, too, and hole up. And when the storm passes, the tracks they leave will be just as clear, maybe a hell of a lot clearer on wet ground."

If they found the tracks again, Longarm reminded himself. They could lose them easily in this place. Hell, you could lose a city in some of these canyons. But he kept his misgivings to himself as he leaned back against the rock, content to stare out at the driving sheets of rain as the lightning flared almost continuously and the side of the canyon reverberated with each maniacal crash of thunder. He'd seen cloudbursts before, but this one was the granddaddy of them all.

"This is your country, Billings," he said. "How long do you think this will last?"

"This here land's been dry for months. It needs a good, long soaking, and this just might be it."

Longarm nodded and puffed on his cheroot for a while before speaking up again. "I keep thinking of that woman passenger. Sally Henderson."

"Sure. I'm thinking of her too. But don't worry. They won't get far. They got problems they don't even know about."

"Problems? What're you talking about?"

He tapped his temple with his forefinger. "They got no imagination."

"You want to spell that out, Sheriff?"

"I've known a few outlaws in my day. From what I've seen, they're brave enough. Some of them. But they never can see far enough ahead to imagine the results of their actions—like kids who set fire to a livery barn then find out what that does to the stock inside and the townsmen afterward," he continued, warming to his topic. "The truth of it is, this trio's robbery of that gold shipment was doomed from the start."

"How come?"

"Like I said, no imagination. Otherwise, they would have figured on the trouble they're going to have lugging around all them sacks of freshly minted gold coins. Have you any idea how difficult it will be for them to transport it, and then to cash it when the time comes? Them poor sonsofbitches might as well be peddling lightning rods in a thunderstorm."

Longarm considered this and found that Billings made good sense.

Expanding on his topic, Billings continued: "Let's assume they get out of these badlands intact. Their horses are going to be done in and they're going to need supplies. So they'll have to flash them freshly minted coins to purchase food and fresh horseflesh. No matter where they go, or how low they tuck their asses, that gold will leave a trace. Like I said, they're doomed."

"I suppose you're right. But I'm still worried about that woman hostage."

"Hell, Long, taking that woman was their worst mistake. Once word gets out they've got a white woman captive, there'll be no place for them to hide."

"If what you say is true," Longarm drawled, "what's to keep them bastards from killing and dumping her in these badlands? You saw the way Sutter flattened her when she tried to get to me."

Billings frowned unhappily. "I admit, that *is* a possibility."

Billings went silent. Leaning back, Longarm pulled his feet in closer to escape the pounding rain and inhaled deeply on his cheroot. The roar from the canyon below them had been increasing steadily and night would soon be on them. As miserable as their present situation was, they were lucky to be up here out of that raging flood surging through the canyon.

Longarm glanced at Billings. "You say you knew some outlaws in your time, Sheriff. That true?"

"That's what I said, ain't it?"

"Ever rob a train?"

"That's a stupid question, Long. You think I'd tell you if I had. I'll just assume you never asked it."

"Just wondering is all. You did mention you'd known some outlaws in your time. Thought you might've known Jesse James or maybe even the Youngers. I sure have read a whole lot about them outlaws."

"Drop the subject, Long."

Billings took a long drag on his cheroot, peering out intently through narrowed eyes at the slanting rain. Longarm's questions appeared to have caused him to draw deeper into himself, even to shrink a little. His expansive and enthusiastic analysis of Sutter's sitation had earlier animated him. Apparently, his annoyance with Longarm's impertinent questions had sobered him.

Maybe, Longarm mused to himself, Billings was thinking of his part in that disastrous gold heist in North Dakota.

The thunder was rising now to a hellish crescendo, effectively choking off any possibility of further conversation. For that Longarm was grateful. He didn't like deceiving Billings, trying to trap him into a damning admission. It was not the way he liked to work. One thing, however, he had already found out: he liked and respected Sheriff Tom Billings.

A series of shattering detonations seemed to tear at the canyon's very foundations. The wind's cry rose to a demented shriek. Peering out from under the rock shelf, Longarm saw the wind-whipped ropes of rain gleaming in the lightning. He edged back farther against the rock face. But it was of little help as the slashing tendrils of rain reached in after him. Before long, he and Billings were completely drenched.

If there was going to be any letup it didn't seem to be near at hand. This miserable day was threatening to become an even more miserable night.

Sally Henderson could not bear Dodger's smell. Nor could she endure his filthy, swinish manner. Unfortunately, when the rising torrent in the canyon forced them to halt and set up camp in this cave out here on the edge of the badlands, Carl Sutter had assigned to her the task of looking after Dodger, warning that if she didn't do her best to fix him up, he really wouldn't have much reason to keep her around.

Her or Dodger.

Sutter's words had terrified her. He had long since convinced her of his casual brutality, and the thought of being abandoned alone in this sodden wasteland with this odious fat man was almost more than she could bear.

Dodger was a bloody mess.

His condition had been worsening steadily, despite the fact that the bullet which had struck him had apparently not broken the bone in his arm. It was the steady loss of blood that was taking its toll, even though Dodger had managed to wrap a crude tourniquet about the wound.

He was sitting now close by the fire, his back propped against the wall of the cave. As Sally cut away his left sleeve with a rusty pair of shears Mary Lou had taken from her saddlebag, he muttered unhappily while sucking on a whiskey bottle. As Sally put down the shears and peeled back the blood-encrusted sleeve, Dodger grinned lewdly at Sally.

She tried not to notice.

With the filthy shirtsleeve off Dodger, she found under it an equally encrusted sleeve of his red long johns. Though she cut around the scabbed wound carefully, it was only with considerable difficulty that she managed to pull the sleeve off the wound. By this time the pain was such that Dodger was no longer grinning at her.

"Damn it!" he whispered hoarsely. "Go easy, woman!"

Sally ignored him as she pulled off both sleeves and flung them into the fire. She looked back at the wound. The campfire's flickering, uncertain light gave her little help, but even so, what she saw was enough to sicken her. The upper forearm had been chewed up badly by the bullet, and in the short time since, a fiery, puckered ridge had grown up around the torn skin. It was an ugly, ragged wound and Sally did not know where to begin if she were to cleanse it thoroughly.

At the same time her stomach was turning queasily, not because of the wound, but because of Dodger's stench, one compounded of his own filthy body and his grimy, unwashed clothes. The man could not have bathed in a fortnight, perhaps even longer. No wonder his wound was becoming septic so quickly.

"Well, woman," Dodger snarled. "Do something, if you're gonna do it."

"I'm going to have to clean out the wound."

"Then do it. I don't want it to get infected. Clean it out and put a fresh bandage on it."

Leaning closer, she noted the ridge of pustulant flesh and broken tissue, not only in the entry wound but in the exit wound in back. Carefully, as gently as she could, she lifted the man's arm to study the wound more closely. A trickle of black, unnatural looking blood was oozing steadily from both fissures.

"It's going to hurt," she told him. "I'll have to open up the wound to get at it."

"Do it, then—but don't be too rough."

Sally got to her feet and took an open saucepan from the fire, threw away what coffee remained in it, then left the cave. Bending her head under the lashing rain, she walked over to a small spring gushing from the side of the slope and filled the pan. Returning to the cave, she placed the saucepan on the fire, then looked about the campsite for a source of bandages. She would need them to swab out the wound, after which she would need clean strips of cloth to close it. But everything her eyes rested on was mud splattered and filthy, or worse.

Sutter and Mary Lou had left the cave, taking their bedrolls with them. What they were doing at the moment did not concern her, though she thought it unlikely they would have been able to find a dry place outside the cave, certainly not in such a terrible, thunderous cloudburst. She looked over at Dodger. She hated and despised the man, but the sight of the pus pullulating from his wound aroused what little sense of humanity still remained within her, despite the example these

81

three execrable human beings set. If she was to help Dodger, she needed bandages.

Her face set grimly, she set out through the driving rain, heading in the direction she had seen the two others take. Eventually she heard voices and found them under a great brow of a rock. They were dry enough, locked in lascivious embrace under a saddle blanket, oblivious to the quaking world around them, and to Sally looming over them.

She cleared her throat.

Sutter lifted himself off Mary Lou and turned his head to scowl up at her. "What the hell do you want, Pretty Pants?"

"I need bandages."

"Why?"

"I must wash out Dodger's wound. It will soon be badly infected if it isn't cleaned out thoroughly. It is already septic, I think."

"Septic?" Sutter demanded. "What the hell is septic?"

"Blood poisoning. He could lose that arm if nothing is done."

"Then go on back and wash it out. Why are you bothering us?"

"I told you. I need bandages, clean bandages." Sally looked at Mary Lou. "Perhaps an old skirt of yours might do."

"There's one in my saddlebag," she told Sally. "Tear it into strips."

"That's right, Pretty Pants," said Sutter, a loathsomely suggestive smile lighting his face. "Take care of Dodger. Be nice to him and maybe he'll cut you in."

"That's right," said Mary Lou, pulling Sutter back

down onto her. Licking her lips, she winked up at Sally. "Take care of your new lover boy and get the hell out of here. We're busy. Or didn't you notice?"

Shocked and angry, Sally flung herself about and charged back through the torrential downpour, on her cheeks tears of outrage mixing with the rain. They did not care a whit for Dodger, or for anyone else, only for their own squalid, obscene pleasures.

When she reached the cave and hurried inside, she saw that Dodger had fallen asleep. Or was he unconscious? She placed the back of her hand against his cheek and found he had a raging fever. As she pulled her hand away and looked about for Mary Lou's saddlebag, Dodger's left hand snaked out and enclosed her left arm in a grip of steel.

He laughed, his foul breath almost overpowering her. He pulled her closer. She struggled to pull herself free of his iron grip, then tried to beat him off, but his strength was frightening, despite the gaping wound in his right arm. By now, she realized, he was half out of his head from his fever, no longer aware of the seriousness of his condition, and no longer caring.

"I'm going to take you, Pretty Pants. Right now. Right here. Yes, I am." He pulled her brutally close and tried to kiss her. She twisted her face away, her stomach heaving.

"You're a sick man!" she cried.

"Hell!" the fat man cried gleefully. "Don't you worry none about that! I feel better already!"

He rolled his enormous bulk over onto her.

"Please!" she cried, her right fist pummeling up at him futilely. "Please! You mustn't do this!"

Again he tried to kiss her. She twisted her face fran-

83

tically from side to side to avoid the horror of his lips closing on hers. The awesome stench of the man was almost overpowering. She could not believe the nightmarish terror of her situation. The world had gone hag. Dodger pressed her still closer to his enormous body; his fat lips pressed wetly on her straining neck. Twisting away, she glimpsed the scissors she had used to cut away his shirtsleeve.

Reaching out, she snatched them up and plunged one of the scissor's blades into Dodger's fleshy back. She was not strong enough to drive it in very deeply, but it was enough to make Dodger roar with pain and pull back off her, the scissors dropping from his back.

Free of his bulk, she jumped to her feet. Dodger uttered a terrible oath and pushed himself erect and lunged for her, furious. She jumped aside to evade his rush, but when she turned to run, her foot struck a boulder in the cave entrance. Unable to regain her balance completely, she tumbled awkwardly down the slope leading from the cave, then sprawled facedown in the mud. A lightning bolt slammed into the earth barely yards from her. At almost the same instant, a terrifying clap of thunder broke just above her head. When a second bolt seared through the atmosphere, turning night into day, she saw Dodger only a few yards from her, ready to pounce.

Far more terrified of him than of the storm, Sally scrambled to her feet and plunged wildly through the demented night. Bushes whipped at her. Trees reared up abruptly in her path, knocking her brutally aside. She slammed into low, ground-hugging boulders. But she kept on. A series of shattering thunderclaps rent the air above her head, seemingly ripping a hole in the clouds as a numbing sluice of water slammed down upon her.

She had difficulty keeping her feet. It was as if the rain were trying to pound her into the ground.

Nevertheless, on she plunged. On her feet one moment, sprawling forward painfully the next, she did not look back once. She did not need to. In her mind's eye Dodger was still close on her heels, still reaching out for her. This awful vision lent wings to her feet, turning her into little more than a small, terrified animal.

Abruptly the ground beneath her opened up. She plunged through space. A rocky outcropping slammed into her side. She tumbled numbly on past it, fell through space for a moment, then came to rest finally on a grassy sward a few feet from the raging torrent surging through the canyon. She drifted in and out of consciousness, only dimly aware of the hammer blows of thunder that rocked the canyon walls.

She became aware of a shadow looming over her. Dodger! She lifted her head in terror, prepared to fling herself into the water. A tongue of lightning played suddenly across the night sky and in its ghostly, flickering light, she saw the single feather thrust upright in the man's headband.

Oh, my God, she thought. An aborigine!

The shock and terror of this night claimed her at last. Her head fell back and she dropped into a numbing, blessed darkness. . . .

Chapter 7

The new day broke clear. Glancing up at the clean heavens, Longarm almost smiled. The morning breeze was cool and fresh. The only reminder of the heavens' titanic tantrum the night before was the steady roar of the torrent sluicing through the canyon below.

After a hasty breakfast of hardtack and jerky, polished off with coffee the sheriff provided and which Longarm considered strong enough to put hair on a doorknob, they mounted up and angled down the slope, heading back to the canyon floor. But the water was still running so high there was no chance of them either following it or crossing to the other side. Any chance of picking up the outlaw's tracks was now out of the question.

Billings glanced back up at the canyon rim. Pointing, he said, "Looks like we'll have to make for the sky and follow along the rim until we pick up their trail."

The climb to the rim was difficult. Their mounts went down more than once as they slipped on the rain-washed gravel and shale. As they clambered higher, the slope, loosened dangerously by the torrential downpour of the night before, quaked and trembled under them. Small ridges broke loose and slid past them. The slope was furrowed by deep runoff channels. Over the last hundred yards to the rim, they were forced to dismount and pull their skittish horses on up after them. Once on the rim, Longarm mounted up and peered around him at the badlands. Small canyons ran off in all directions; some became larger, others more narrow, and still others dwindled to narrow ravines and gorges.

Longarm suddenly had little hope that they would ever find Sutter in this labyrinthine wasteland. He said nothing of the sort to Billings, however, and let the man take the lead. He did so unhappily, it seemed, his face grim with resolve.

About ten o'clock that morning, they rounded a bluff and found themselves facing a line of four mounted Ute Indians. An ancient warrior with two upright eagle feathers in his black Stetson's hatband raised his hand in greeting to Billings, who held up his hand in greeting, also.

As Billings nudged his horse forward to meet the old chief, Longarm kept his own horse alongside. Billings pulled up before the old warrior.

"The sheriff of Rimrock is pleased to look upon his old friend," Billings said.

With the faintest trace of a smile on his wrinkled face, the chief replied, "The heart of Running Fox soars to see the famous sheriff of Rimrock."

"What the hell're you doin' out here in plain sight,

Chief?" Billings demanded, abruptly dispensing with formality. "You know you better keep yourselves hid."

"It is not easy to stay invisible in the land of one's ancestors."

"Damn it, Chief. You know if your people keep poppin' up like this, someone's liable to send the horse soldiers to gather you up and make you live with your brothers."

"Let the horse soldiers come. Once again we will become invisible." The old Indian glanced at Longarm. "And who is this one?"

"He's just helpin' me out. He was on a stage got held up."

"We know of this. Now you chase the outlaws. There is much gold. Whites go crazy for gold. These outlaws are evil men. They stink up the land of our ancestors. But you, my old friend, are like the dog who has lost his nose."

Billings sighed. "That's about the way I figured it myself, Chief. Which way did the bastards go?"

The Indian pointed to a ridge to the northwest. Longarm realized they had passed that same ridge an hour ago. Running Fox was telling them they were going the wrong way. He and the rest of his band had come out to help the sheriff keep the sacred land of their ancestors free of cockroaches like Carl Sutter and Mary Lou.

Billings turned to Longarm. "You got another one of them cheroots?"

Longarm reached into his jacket's inside pocket for one and handed it to Billings, who passed it on to the chief. The chief took it with what passed for a smile—a slight rearrangement of the myriad wrinkles on his face.

After a close examination of the thin cigar, he looked with twinkling eyes at Longarm.

"Running Fox rides with three fine braves. Like him, they are great hunters and warriors. They like good smoke, too."

Longarm reached again into his pocket and pulled out three more cheroots. At this rate, he'd soon run out, he realized. Running Fox rode back to the other braves, passed out the cheroots, and then, without a backward glance, the four Ute Indians lifted their ponies to a lope and rode off.

"Let's go," said Billings, turning his horse toward the ridge Running Fox had pointed out. "That old piss pot has saved my ass again."

"He does that often, does he?" Longarm asked, turning his horse also.

"I return the favor, Long. Every chance I get. And I'm supposed to report to the army any sightings of Mountain Ute in the vicinity."

"But you don't."

"You're damn right I don't. This here was their land long before the army took it. Besides, put an Indian inside an agency and you take out his heart."

"Like putting a man in jail."

"Precisely."

"You ever been in jail?"

"You ask too damn many questions, Long."

"If you don't ask questions, you don't find out anything."

"What are you trying to find out, Long?"

"Right now, where them outlaws are heading."

"Looks like the valley northwest of the badlands. They might even be heading for Mountain City. If they are, they'll end up delivering that gold for us."

Billings lifted his horse to a lope and Longarm followed suit.

Carl Sutter shook Mary Lou insistently. Despite the storm's fury the night before and all the trouble with Dodger, she had fallen asleep without a murmur. She was one hell of a woman, Sutter realized as he stood back and watched her stir drowsily. She would pleasure a man in broad daylight with the whole world watching, then sleep like a babe afterward.

Yawning, Mary Lou sat up, scratched her head and stared blearily at him. "We got to get going this early?"

"Damn right we do. We got them two on our trail, don't forget."

"Maybe they lost us in the storm."

"We can't count on that."

She considered that for a minute, then nodded in agreement. The sleep drained out of her immediately, it seemed, as she came alive. She flung aside her blanket and stood up as naked as a plucked chicken and went looking for a place to pee.

When she came back, Sutter had a fire going. She dressed quickly, then took out the saucepan and made some coffee, then fried some beans and bacon. While it was sizzling, Sutter hunkered down beside her.

"I took a ride earlier," he said. "There's a valley not too far ahead of us, once we get out of these badlands. The horses are fine. No pack sores. I've already grained and watered them."

"Where'll that valley take us?"

"No place special. Mountain City's a good three days' ride farther on."

"You sure?"

"That's where it was the last time I rode through here."

Behind them, just inside the cave, Dodger whimpered, then groaned. Sutter and Mary Lou turned to glance at him. Dodger was in such discomfort, he hardly noticed them.

Mary Lou glanced covertly at Sutter. "What about Sam? He's hurt bad, and he ain't in no mood to help much, not with Pretty Pants gone."

"Did you see that hole she left in his back?"

"He came whining to me last night in the middle of the storm. She never struck nothin' fatal, not with that hide of his to get through."

"Yeah. But his feelin's are hurt."

"So what do we do with him?"

"We leave him."

"Suppose he don't want to stay behind?"

Sutter patted his six-gun.

"Then do it. Now."

"After we eat, for Christ's sake. What's your hurry?"

"You out of your mind? What do you think woke him up? The smell of bacon frying. Get rid of him now or I'll have to fix us another breakfast."

Sutter got up and walked into the cave. Dodger was still not fully awake and was lying back on his bed of pine boughs. Bending over the fat man, Sutter took out his revolver and nudged Doger in the shoulder with the barrel. Dodger moved restlessly under the prodding, but did not sit up. Sutter pulled back and straightened up, his eyes filled with disgust as he contemplated the sodden mass of flesh stretched out before him.

He didn't particularly like what he was about to do,

but Mary Lou was in agreement. There was no way Dodger was going to agree to being left behind. And there was sure as hell no reason for keeping Dodger with them. In his condition he would only hold them back. Maybe he better not wake Dodger up, not if he was going to have to kill the poor slob anyway.

"Grub's ready," Mary Lou called. She sounded impatient.

Sutter swallowed. "Be right there," he told her. "Keep your shirt on."

He took a step back to get a better angle on Dodger's head and cocked his gun. Abruptly, Dodger came fully awake and pushed himself up onto his elbows. Sutter quickly dropped his gun hand to his side.

Confused, Dodger stared at Sutter. "Was that you pokin' me?"

"Yeah."

Dodger's moon face brightened. "Food's on. I can smell it. Jesus, I'm hungry."

He pushed himself ponderously upright and stood swaying in the cave entrance. His left shirtsleeve had been cut away, and from his wound on down his arm was sheathed in dried blood. It looked like hell.

"Stay right there, Dodger," Sutter told him. "I got something to tell you."

"So tell me."

Sutter glanced toward the campfire. Mary Lou was on her feet, watching. If he showed any weakness or lack of resolve now, he realized, she would never let him live it down.

"We both decided, Dodger. You're staying behind."

"What d'you mean, staying behind?"

"We're going to have to leave you here, Dodger. You

ain't no good to us. Not with that wound and that hole in your back!"

"Hell, you can't run out on me now!"

"Sure I can." Sutter lifted his revolver, cocked it, aimed, and pulled the trigger.

The gun misfired.

With a howl of rage, Dodger flung himself out of the cave at Sutter. Both men crashed to the ground, Dodger on top. Lights exploded in Sutter's skull. He thought he heard a rib cracking. Somehow, he managed to thumb-cock and squeeze the trigger again. This time the gun fired, the detonation muffled by Dodger's bulk. With a howl of pain, Dodger flipped back off Sutter, tried to stand up, lost his balance and tumbled about ten feet down the slope where he slid to a halt, facedown in the mud.

Getting to his feet, Sutter wiped off the mud that clung to him, picked up his hat and clapped it back on. Cautiously, he walked down the slope to inspect Dodger. Halting beside him, Sutter watched the downed man warily, hs gun cocked and waiting. When Dodger did not move, Sutter kicked him viciously in the side at the spot where he thought his bullet might have entered. When the body lifted under the force of the blow, he glimpsed a dark flood gouting from the wound.

Satisfied, Sutter hurried over to join Mary Lou, who was already saddling their horses. They could always eat later.

Josh burst into the kitchen. "Lone Bear!" he shouted. "He's come back! And he's got someone!"

Jenny dropped the ladle she had been using to stir the pot of blueberry preserves and lifted the pot off the stove; then, wiping her hands on her apron, she followed Josh out onto the front porch. From the direction of the chicken coop where Annie had gone to grain the chickens, Annie came running too.

Shading her eyes, Jenny saw Lone Bear astride his pony crossing the shallow stream, someone sitting on his pommel, facing him. When he rode closer, she could see it was a woman, her long hair spilling down her back as she rested her head against Long Bear's massive chest. She did not move as Lone Bear passed the barn and headed for the ranch house. Jenny hurried down the porch steps.

Before she reached Lone Bear, he swung out of his saddle, holding the woman in his arms as easily as if she were made of straw. She was barely conscious and moaned softly as Lone Bear carried her toward Jenny. Jenny saw at once what a pitiful condition she was in. Her arms, face and neck were scratched and bloodied, her skirts torn, her blouse ripped and soiled beyond repair. And she was covered with bruises.

Jenny stepped back out of Lone Bear's way. "Take her into my bedroom," she told him. "It's the one at the end of the hall just beyond the kitchen."

Without a word, Lone Bear mounted the porch steps and entered the ranch house, Jenny and the two children following close behind. Josh and Annie were wise enough to contain their excitement. Though they were glad to see Lone Bear, they realized that he had returned not to see them, but to help someone who appeared to be seriously injured.

Following down the short hall, Jenny entered her bedroom behind Lone Bear and watched as the Indian

95

put the woman gently down on the bed, then stepped aside to let Jenny examine her.

Jenny stepped quickly forward and found that the woman was now completely unconscious. Though it appeared she had no open wounds or broken bones, Jenny was concerned she might have internal injuries. Her legs and knees were battered fearfully; there were several lacerations on her head and a sharp cut under one ear. Jenny judged the woman to be in her early twenties—and something about her was vaguely familiar. And then she remembered. This was the woman from the East Jenny had met briefly in the hotel lobby in Rimrock. She had been planning to take the stage to Mountain City.

"Ma? Who's that?"

Jenny turned to see Josh and Annie standing in her bedroom doorway, wide-eyed.

"Her name is Sally Henderson."

"Is she going to die?"

"Of course not. Now go back outside and play," she told them. "Josh, you keep an eye on your sister."

Josh and Annie were not happy at being dismissed so peremptorily, but they were obedient children. They turned and left the room, Josh holding Annie's hand firmly in his.

Jenny looked at Lone Bear for an explanation.

"This woman come through badlands with three other whites. These whites are bad. Their packhorses carry very heavy load. Gold, I think. It is always gold that makes whites kill and rob."

"But I know this woman," Jenny told him. "She was supposed to have taken a stage from Rimrock the day before."

"Running Fox tell me three white men rob stage and take this woman. In the night, she flee from one of the men and run like crazy horse and fall down cliff. When I find her, she see me and faint like the pampered English women in your novels. But maybe she is hurt bad. So I take her to you."

Jenny looked back at Sally Henderson. "I'll need some hot water and bandages to wash her off," she told Lone Bear. "I'll need to do that to find out how badly she's been hurt."

"I will go into the kitchen and build a fire in the stove."

"There is one already. Just put a large pot of water on to boil."

He left the room, and only after he had done so did she realize how easily she had given Lone Bear instructions. She was certain this was not the way a woman treated an Indian male, and for just an instant she was flustered, wondering if she might not have offended him.

But there was no time for such considerations now. She leaned over the woman and found her returning to consciousness.

"Sally," Jenny called softly, "can you hear me?"

The woman's eyes opened, gazed foggily up at the ceiling, then focused on Jenny. "You know me?" she asked, her voice barely above a hoarse whisper.

"Of course. Don't you remember me? I'm Jenny Wills. We met in the hotel in Rimrock."

Sally's face lit. "Oh, yes. I remember."

"You're at my ranch now. Lone Bear found you and brought you here."

"I know," she whispered, her eyes searching the

room nervously. "The aborigine. Where is he? I thought he was going to—"

"You were perfectly safe at all times, Sally. I assure you. Lone Bear is a very intelligent and kind man, a member of the Mountain Utes."

"Then I'm safe."

"Perfectly."

"I can't believe it."

"How badly are you hurt?"

"I'm sore all over."

"Have you broken any bones, do you think?"

Carefully, gingerly, Sally moved her limbs and arms, tensing for any sign of pain sharp enough to tell her that they were not functioning properly. At the conclusion of the test, she smiled in some relief at Jenny.

"Nothing is broken. At least, I don't think so."

"Lone Bear said you fell from a cliff."

"Yes. There was a storm. I was running from a . . . terrible man."

"What man?"

"Dodger. He was repulsive. He was so fat and he stank so." She shuddered at his memory. "All three were horrid. They stopped the stage and robbed it. They killed the stage driver and the young boy with the shotgun. Later, they took the gold hidden in the floor." She shook her head, frowning, as if she found it impossible to believe. "It's all like a hideous nightmare."

Jenny realized how right Lone Bear was. Gold did make white men mad. "The nightmare's over, Sally," Jenny told her comfortingly. "You're safe now, a good distance from the badlands, and I am sure all those outlaws can think of right now is escaping with their gold."

"Yes. I . . . suppose that is true, isn't it."

The fear left Sally's eyes; her face lost its tension. She closed her eyes and took a long breath, and before Jenny had a chance to suggest she sleep, she fell into a deep, profound slumber.

Jenny hurried from the room to get a pan of water and some washcloths, and without awakening Sally, she managed to wash off the mud and dried blood that still clung to her body. What Jenny found in the process was encouraging. There were many cuts, but none were more than skin deep, and though the bruises were certainly not pleasant to look upon, Jenny had little doubt that Sally would recover nicely.

She dressed the sleeping woman in her nightgown, tucked her snugly under the covers, and stole from the bedroom. She found Lone Bear asleep at the table, his head resting on his folded arms.

Gently, she shook him awake.

"She's going to be all right, Lone Bear," she told him. "There were no serious injuries. That terrible fall she took didn't help any, but I'm sure she'll soon be up and about."

Lone Bear got to his feet. "That is good." He looked in the direction of the bedroom and smiled. "She was very much afraid of me. She think I take her away to my lodge to scalp her. I will go now."

"Be careful, Lone Bear."

"You too, Jenny Wills. Those crazy whites bring death with them. And they are still out there."

They walked to the front door together and she stepped out onto the porch with him. The sudden, unexpected arrival of Sally Henderson had taken most of the morning from her. It must already be past nine, she realized, noting how high the sun had climbed already.

The children were playing in a favorite patch of bare ground under a willow. She could see the stream's waters winking at her through the cottonwoods beyond.

Lone Bear descended the short flight of porch steps and swung onto his pony. "Remember what I say, Jenny Wills. Be careful."

The powerful timbre of his voice as he pronounced her name sent a tremor down her spine. Shading her eyes from the low sun, she watched him turn his pony and ride out of the compound. Seeing him leave, Josh and Annie stood up to wave.

He returned their wave and before long was splashing across the shallow stream, heading back toward the badlands. She watched him go until he was out of sight. It was with a strange feeling of emptiness that she turned and went back inside. But she shook off the feeling and reminded herself that she still had blueberry preserves to bottle.

She hurried down the hall to the kitchen.

Chapter 8

Dodger was not dead yet.

The moment he felt Sutter's bullet rip into his side, he realized he was in bad trouble and allowed himself to tumble on down the slope past him. After coming to rest facedown in the mud, he heard Sutter approach and waited tensely, not daring to breathe. He could feel Sutter standing over him and expected at any moment to hear the cock of his revolver and feel another slug tear into him. His only hope, he realized, was for Sutter to think he was already dead. When Sutter kicked him in the side, it was all he could do not to cry out.

After Sutter moved off, Dodger remained on the slope, fearful that at any moment Sutter might return. His senses were reeling. A furnacelike heat raged inside his body. He was just about ready to get to his feet and make a run for it when he heard Mary Lou approaching with Sutter to inspect what they thought was Dodger's corpse.

Mary Lou poked Dodger judiciously with her foot, then stepped back quickly, as if he were a dangerous rattler. He kept himself from reacting and could hear Mary Lou talking to Sutter. Her words were not kind. She called him a pig, said she was glad to be rid of him and urged Sutter to put another bullet into him to make sure. But Sutter said they didn't have the time. As they turned finally and left him in the mud, he heard Mary Lou's sudden bright trill of laughter, and was filled with desolation. No rebuke had ever cut him as cruelly as the sound of that heartless laughter.

For an interminable time, Dodger waited for them to pull out, and only when the last packhorse dropped from sight did he dare push himself upright. The wound in his gut burned like a branding iron. Hot blood pulsed from it, issuing down his leg, dribbling into his boot. He struggled back up the slope, found his hat, and after considerable effort managed to saddle and mount his horse. He checked to make sure his Sharps was in its saddle scabbard, then pointed the horse down the slope after them.

He had not gone far before he realized he had to do something about the thigh wound. Pulling to a halt, he lowered his gun belt and snugged it tight over the entry wound. This slowed the blood a little and he started up again. By this time the pain rocketing up through his gut made his head pound. Sutter's bullet must have ranged deep into his bowels. Meanwhile, his left arm was useless, and a gray cloud kept passing before his eyes.

He was sure as hell in no condition to take after them two. Maybe the best thing for him to do would be to find a place to die. A cool place. Some grass alongside an icy cold mountain stream. He could duck his head into it and cool himself off.

That might be the best thing, but he couldn't do it. He was worth more than them two, and he was going to get them if it was the last thing he ever did. Their treatment of him had roused him as had nothing else in his life. It wasn't the bullet or the kicks, the general meanness—it was that final cruel laugh of Mary Lou's. He could still hear it as he rode and it goaded him on as nothing else could. He would live long enough to overtake them both and bring them down with his Sharps.

He kept on grimly.

When he finally glimpsed Sutter and Mary Lou, he was still high in the rocks and they were below him, leading their packhorses out into a lush, grass-carpeted valley. He could ride no farther. If he did not get them now, they would escape him for good.

Slipping awkwardly off his horse, he snaked the Sharps from its scabbard and lurched toward a low boulder. Reaching it, he braced himself, gasping. He estimated them to be less than five hundred yards away, still well within range of the Sharps. He had some difficulty loading and aiming the Sharps and could barely hold it steady. Gritting his teeth, he lifted the heavy barrel and forced his left hand to brace it as he lined up the sights. The pain in his left arm made his head swim, but he concentrated mightily, ignoring the beads of dirty sweat which dropped from his eyebrows and stung his eyes. When the rifle's sights rested finally on Carl Sutter's back, Dodger pulled the trigger.

The Sharps's powerful recoil rocked Dodger back. He almost fell, but grabbed the edge of the boulder and pulled himself upright. His shot had missed, but the sound of it had caused Sutter and Mary Lou to lift their horses to a lope, dragging the overloaded packhorses behind them. Cursing, no longer mindful of the pain, Dodger reloaded, tracked more carefully this time, and allowing for drift, squeezed off his second shot. This time, he did not allow the recoil to slam him back, and clinging to the boulder, he waited.

A packhorse stumbled and went down.

Sutter and Mary Lou, lashing their horses, loped deeper into the valley, the two remaining packhorses barely able to stay on their feet as they were dragged after them.

Dodger groaned. Sutter and Mary Lou were now out of range. And he was a dead man.

"Aw, shit," he muttered.

He sagged backward, turned, and using the Sharps as a crutch, staggered toward his horse. He had not gone more than a few yards before he plunged blindly to the ground. He felt it tipping crazily under him. He lifted his head once, then lay back.

His horse had looked up nervously at his erratic approach. Its ears flattened skittishly and it shook its head. When Dodger hit the ground and lay still, the horse waited a while, then lowered its head and resumed cropping the grass at its feet, drifting slowly away as it followed the sparse growth.

Sutter pulled up and looked back at the rocks. Mary Lou reined in also and turned her horse. The packhorses staggered to a halt also, shaking their heads and blowing.

"That was a Sharps," Sutter said. "Dodger's."

"That's what I figured."

"Damn it! I thought I killed him."

Mary Lou said nothing.

"He must be finished now," Sutter said hopefully, squinting up at the rocks, looking for a glint of sunlight off a gun barrel. "He would've kept on firing if he wasn't."

"We're out of range," Mary Lou pointed out. "That's why he stopped."

"Not with that Sharps, we ain't. A man ain't hardly ever out of range of that rifle."

Mary Lou looked at Sutter with barely disguised contempt. Sutter's statement was silly. No rifle, not even a Sharps, could hit what a dying fat man could not see. "I say we go back for the gold."

"You sure that's such a good idea?"

"You want to leave all that gold?"

"No, damn it, I don't."

"Let's go, then."

They rode back to the fallen horse. Ignoring the dying horse's thrashing, they transferred the gold to the two remaining packhorses. Mounting up again, Sutter glanced back over his shoulder at the rocks, as if he were still expecting Dodger to open up on them again.

Then he wrapped the lead reins about his saddle horn and led the way on across the valley. The rain the night before had softened the ground, and as they rode the packhorses found the footing a problem. In addition, they were now carrying even more of the gold than they had been carrying before.

Glancing back at the laboring animals, Mary Lou suggested to Sutter that they go slower, that they were asking too much of the horses. But Sutter was unwilling to slow down and, ignoring her suggestion, spurred his horse on without pause.

Longarm pulled up and glanced at Billings. "You hear that?"

"I heard it."

They were staring at a rock outcropping on the horizon. The shot had come from that direction. Then came a second crack, its echo ringing among the distant rocks.

Billings looked shrewdly at Longarm. "Thieves falling out?"

"Maybe."

"Sure. All that gold. No outlaw wants to share his take."

They put their horses into motion. As they crossed a sodden clearing farther on, they caught sight of fresh tracks. Billings jumped down to study them. Longarm pulled his horse to a halt alongside Billings.

Billings straightened up. "Five horses. Three of them overloaded," he told Longarm. "That means three packhorses to carry all that gold, Sally Henderson, and only two outlaws. The female and Sutter. They must've dumped the fat man somewhere. And maybe Sally, too."

"Maybe that's what the firing's about."

"Could be."

Billings swung up into his saddle. Following the tracks, they splashed across the wet ground. They saw at once that the tracks would take them to that distant pile of rocks on the horizon, the spot from which those two shots had come.

A mile or so farther on, as they neared the rocks,

they caught sight of a saddled horse cropping grass near the base of the ridge. When they got closer, they saw that the horse was standing alongside a narrow trail that led up into the rocks. Dismounting alongside it, Longarm caught up the dragging reins and examined the horse and the saddle. The blood had not quite dried on the saddle skirts, and the rifle scabbard was empty.

Billings dismounted. The two men drew their weapons and continued on foot up the narrow trail to a ridge that overlooked the lush valley beyond. At once they spotted heavy, lurching bootprints gouged out of the soft ground. Following them, they rounded a boulder and almost stumbled over Dodger's body. Billings hopped around to the other side of it and leaned cautiously over the still form.

"Looks like you're right," Longarm drawled. "The Dodger's not going to get his share of the take."

A Sharps rifle lay beside the body. Longarm picked it up. The muzzle was clogged with mud, but he could smell the trace of recently fired gunpowder. It must have been Dodger who had fired those two shots.

Looking down at him, Billings nudged the big fellow in the side with the tip of his boot. He thought he heard a groan. Frowning, he bent closer. Dodger rolled over, a smile on his mud-streaked face, a .44 Colt double-action in his right hand. Before he could fire, Longarm kicked the revolver out of his hand. As the gun struck a rock embedded in the ground, it fired, the bullet taking a piece out of Billings's vest.

Billings drew his own revolver and covered the fat man.

"Go ahead. Pull the trigger," Dodger gasped. "I'm dead already."

Billings holstered his weapon and glanced at Longarm. "Thanks," he said.

"Now we're even, Billings."

They looked back down at the Dodger. He was still staring up at them. But he didn't see them now, not them or anyone else.

Longarm walked over and picked up his .44 the Dodger had slipped out of his rig in the stagecoach. It looked none the worse for the wear. He withdrew Dodger's own Colt and dropped it beside the dead man. He had not liked its balance and was glad to get his own weapon back. He'd have liked to get that derringer and watch back also. But he didn't see how he could be *that* lucky.

Dropping his .44 back into his cross-draw rig, he saw that the dead man's tracks led from a boulder sitting on the brow of the ridge. He followed the tracks to the boulder, then gazed down at the valley below. It was a pleasant enough prospect, the high, lush grass stretching clear to the horizon.

Billings joined him.

"I wonder if the Dodger hit what he aimed at," Longarm muttered as his gaze swept slowly over the valley floor.

"I see something," said Billings.

So did Longarm, something dark lying in the grass. It was large enough to be a horse. He glanced skyward. Two buzzards rocked like cinders in the updraft high above. Before long, Longarm guessed, they would be dropping for the feast.

"Looks like the fat man's Sharps did hit something after all," Longarm said.

"Let's go," replied Billings.

Sutter yanked yard and swore. The packhorse straightened up and regained its balance, then went down again, more heavily this time, as if the quagmire into which it had stumbled had swallowed it up. The animal lifted its head and thrashed frantically in an effort to regain its feet. But in its weakened state the inexorable weight of all that gold packed onto its back would not allow it. The horse gave up and lay back on its side, its forelegs pawing feebly.

Mary Lou dropped the reins of the two packhorses she was leading, turned her horse, and rode closer to the foundering beast. Sutter had dismounted the moment the packhorse had sank into the mud. Now he strode angrily toward it.

"I told you we were going too fast," Mary Lou told him, dismounting as well. "I told you we better give these horses a chance to rest, some water, at least."

"We don't have any water."

"Look over there, you damn fool. There's a line of trees on the horizon. Cottonwoods and willows. That means water. All we had to do was be patient."

Sutter shaded his eyes and saw the trees, then glanced over at her. "Why the hell didn't you tell me?"

"I just saw them myself. But you were in such a sweat, we might've missed them, gone right on past, if this horse hadn't given up on us. It's finished now, Carl. It won't go an inch farther."

"Shut up," he snapped. "We'll just have to carry some of the gold ourselves."

Mary Lou steadied her mount with a pat on its neck. "From now on, I say we go slower."

"Do you now?"

"Yes."

He glared at her, hating her for always getting the last word. And for being right, as usual. She saw the hate blaze in his eyes and gave it right back to him—in spades.

Sutter saw the steel in her gaze and decided he might as well back off for now. "Okay," he said. "Okay. So I pushed this packhorse too hard."

"Like you say, our horses can carry some of the gold, but not all of it. We'll soon be walking if we try that."

"You mean we got to leave some of this gold behind?"

"Some of it. Bury it along the bank of that river. We can come back for it later."

"I don't like it. We might never get back here."

"Then carry it yourself, on your horse. Put the extra gold in your saddlebags. Not mine."

"Then I'd lose my own horse and you'd keep on going."

"If you act like a fool, you deserve to be treated like one."

He looked at her sullenly. Someday he'd get his chance. Someday. "All right. We'll head for that river, water our horses and fill our canteens. Then we'll bury what gold we can't carry."

Sutter went back for his mount. Mary Lou dismounted and began untying the aparejos still strapped onto the feebly thrashing horse. Once she had pulled them free, she began extracting the coin-filled pouches. Sutter joined her and they transferred the bulk of the gold to their saddlebgs. It was hot, wearing work.

Not until this very moment had they imagined how formidable a task it would be for them to transport this much gold over open country.

After nursing their rapidly weakening horses to the stream, a distance that turned out to be close to four miles, they glanced across the lazy water at the ranch house and barns visible through the trees on the other side. They were close enough to hear the chickens clucking.

They glanced at each other, grinning like coyotes.

"Hot damn!" Sutter cried, dismounting quickly and leading his horse to the stream bank. "Do you see what I see?"

"A ranch house. And barns," she said, chuckling. "And listen to them hens. That means fresh eggs."

"And look at them horses in the corral behind the barn. What's that about us havin' to walk? Mary Lou, we just found us all we goin' to need."

Mary Lou dismounted. "Damn it if you ain't right. We sure are lucky. I was beginning to think Dodger had done us in with that last shot."

Leading her horse to the water, Mary Lou took a deep breath and peered through the trees. She didn't see any menfolk around, and something about the appearance of the place told her they wouldn't find any. Even so, she and Carl could handle any men who tried to stop them.

From the look of things, she was certain they would find all the fresh horseflesh they needed, and plenty of fresh provisions too. She sighed deeply in relief. Carl

Sutter was a fool, and for a while there she had been worried that nothing was going to turn out as they had planned it.

Sally Henderson awoke to the sound of birds. She sat up and glanced out the window. The sun was high, the world bright. Chickens were clucking somewhere. She felt sore all over, as if she had fallen down a flight of stairs. But when she flipped aside the covers, she realized she was still intact, and eased herself carefully up onto her feet. Slippers had been placed beside the bed. She slipped her bare feet into them, pushed open the bedroom door, moved cautiously down the short hall, and came out into the kitchen.

A young boy was just pushing through the back door with an armload of kindling. He pulled up short when he saw Sally. A little girl not much older than four was sitting at the table, her back to Sally, paring a bowl full of potatoes. She was so tiny, her mother had piled books up onto the chair to get her high enough. At the kitchen sink, standing alongside the hand pump, the woman she knew as Jenny was washing off a recently plucked chicken.

Josh moved on into the kitchen and dumped the kindling into the wood box beside the black iron stove squatting in the corner. As he did so, Jenny turned and caught sight of Sally standing in the kitchen doorway.

"Sally!"

"I just woke up. It was the birds."

"But you need to rest."

"No, I'm fine," Sally insisted gently, moving into the kitchen. "But don't mind me. Just go ahead with what you're doing. I'll just sit down over here at the table."

Josh, staring up at Sally, went slowly back outside for more kindling. Little Annie piped up. "Are you going to live with us now?"

"Yes, she will," Jenny told her. "For a while, anyway."

"That's very kind of you," Sally told her. "I really have nowhere to turn until I reach Mountain City. All my luggage is gone, my things scattered everywhere."

"How awful. You're lucky to have escaped them. Do you remember much about last night?"

"Only the terrible storm, and fleeing, and then that aborigine."

"His name's Lone Bear."

"Oh, yes. You told me this morning, I remember."

"He's a very fine man."

"I suppose he . . . saved my life, didn't he."

"That's quite probable. I don't think you would have lasted long out there alone. And then, of course, that man who was chasing you might have found you."

"Yes," Sally agreed, shuddering, "he might have."

"But we don't need to talk about that any more," Jenny told her. "All that is behind you." She smiled then. "And I could use some company."

"Could I help some now?"

"You mean stay out here in the kitchen?"

"Yes. It would seem so normal, so perfectly peaceful really, after all I've been through."

Jenny laughed. "I suppose it would at that."

She reached into the sink and lifted out of it a freshly washed bowl of carrots and placed them down on the table before Sally, then handed her a paring knife. As Sally pulled the bowl of carrots toward her and began

113

scraping the carrots clean, Jenny dried her hands and sat down at the table to join her.

"Why don't you let Annie play outside," Sally suggested, "so the two of us old hens can gossip?"

"Annie," Jenny suggested, "would you like to go out and play with Josh?"

Annie dropped her paring knife into the bowl and nodded quickly.

Jenny took the bowl from her. "Then scoot."

With a grateful glance at Sally, Annie slipped down from her perch and burst out the kitchen door, calling to Josh as she did so.

"You've made a friend for life," Jenny said, laughing.

Jenny Wills was not beautiful, Sally decided, but she had something far more exciting than beauty, a vibrant, active intelligence. It glowed in her face and eyes with the warmth of sunlight.

Sally glanced appreciatively about the kitchen. "This is such a warm, cozy place. Do you and the children live here alone, Jenny?"

"Since my husband died, yes."

"Oh, I'm sorry. When was that?"

"Two years ago. The cholera took him. Some settlers passed through the valley on the way to California and stayed with us for a while. James would not think of them going on at the time, the weather in the mountains was so bad. When they pushed on at last, they left us with the cholera. All of us got fearfully sick, but it was James the sickness took."

"That must have been terrible for you."

"James was always a frail, gentle man, but he was strong in so many ways. And he did so love the children. But sometimes I felt he was not up to living in the West. He would much rather read a book or write a poem than chase some cattle rustler off our range." She sighed and looked at Sally. "And you, what about you, Sally? Are you on your way to meet your husband?"

Sally blushed. "Far from it, I'm afraid. I am on my way to Mountain City to meet a school committee. I've been offered a position as a schoolteacher."

Jenny looked closely at Sally. "Just then I caught something in your eyes. If you don't want to tell me about it, you don't have to." She smiled. "But I'm a good listener."

Sally laughed softly and picked up a carrot. "Oh, yes, there was a man, sure enough. A cad, really. I was terribly hurt when he broke our engagement. So I came West. I was such a fool."

"Yes," Jenny said with a gentle smile, "I guess you were. And from what I hear about Mountain City, you've jumped from the frying pan into the fire."

"That's what I've been hearing."

"Of course, you shouldn't let yourself be discouraged. We do need teachers out here—and women. I, for one, am glad you came. Mountain City is a few days' ride. But that isn't so far out here. Perhaps we can become friends."

Sally placed her hand on Jenny's. "We already are, Jenny."

Josh burst in then with still more kindling, Annie following up behind him with a few well-chosen pieces of kindling herself. It was clear the two were anxious to check in on their mother and get another look at her visitor. Strangers were a rarity in this country, especially

115

women who were carried in unconscious early in the morning by their Indian friend Lone Bear.

"That's fine, children," Jenny told them. "We've got plenty of wood for supper now. Go on outside and play for a while."

They left, not reluctantly, but not very quickly, either.

"Jenny, aren't you afraid to be out here like this? I mean, without a man around. This is such wild country."

"We're not really alone."

"You mean the Indians?"

"Yes. The Utes. They look after us, you might say."

"And you're not afraid of them? That they might go . . . on the warpath?"

Jenny laughed, delighted. "Those days are gone, Sally. The poor Indians are locked up in federal agencies now, except for the few Apaches well south of here that have managed to elude the army. If you want the truth of it, I am more afraid of white men than I am of an Indian. If you treat an Indian fairly, he will never betray you. You can't always say that of a white man."

Sally thought of Lone Bear then. If he had not brought her to Jenny's ranch, she would still be out there now somewhere in that terrible land, at the mercy of those outlaws.

"I'll take your word for it, Jenny," Sally said. She finished slicing a carrot and reached for another. "But you can imagine what I've read back East. Some call them God's natural children. Others insist they are cruel savages, heathen aborigines who must be exterminated if this land is to be made safe for Christians."

Jenny frowned thoughtfully. "I suppose the truth lies

somewhere in between. But it seems to me you usually find in people what you expect to find."

Josh burst into the kitchen, Annie on his heels. "Someone's coming!" he cried. "They just rode in!"

Sally and Jenny hurried to the window. Sally gasped. Mary Lou and Carl Sutter had left their horses and were running hard for the kitchen door. They must have seen the children burst inside. A second later, guns drawn, they slammed into the kitchen and came to a halt, grinning.

And Sally found herself back in her nightmare.

Chapter 9

The suddenness of their entrance and the cold glint in the intruders' eyes were enough to terrify little Annie. She began to whimper. Josh, his chin square, reached out and pulled her close.

Sally placed herself between the children and the outlaws. "Don't harm these people," she told them. "Please. If you want, I'll go with you. Only don't harm them."

"What the hell makes you think we'd want you to come with us?" Mary Lou said. "Dodger is dead. We don't need you to keep him busy."

"Horses," Sutter told Jenny. "We need horses—fresh mounts and packhorses. And provisions. Ain't no reason for any trouble, long as you don't give us any. Where's the menfolk? We couldn't find none out there."

"There are none," Jenny said coldly. "The horses are

in the barn. Take what provisions you need from the kitchen here."

"I'll bring in some of those extra saddlebags," Sutter told Mary Lou. "Start emptying them cupboards." He glanced at Jenny. "How many horses you got out there."

"Six. But one's a mare with foal."

"We'll take them all," he told her, still smiling. "But don't worry, we'll leave you our horses. They might be a little worn out, but hell, you won't be goin' nowhere for a while."

He vanished out the door. Mary Lou holstered her enormous Colt and, brushing past Jenny, stepped up onto a chair and opened the cupboard doors. Jenny had already laid up a winter's store of preserves, and on her recent trip to Rimrock had purchased enough canned goods to see her through the fall and winter. These Mary Lou swiftly transferred to the kitchen table. Sutter reentered, lugging four empty saddlebags and a knapsack for Mary Lou.

As Sutter left the kitchen, Sally saw the dismay on Jenny's face at the amounts Mary Lou was stuffing into the saddlebags. When Sutter returned with more saddlebags, Sally stepped angrily into his path.

"You're taking everything!" she told him. "You can't do this! You must leave her food for the children."

"Let her kill some chickens," Sutter snarled. "Get out of my way."

He brushed Sally aside so roughly she lost her balance. She grabbed at the edge of the table, missed, and crashed to the floor, her head thudding loudly. With startling suddenness Josh left his sister and exploded across the room at Sutter, his head slamming into the man's stomach and driving him back against the sink.

As the breath exploded out of him, his face went gray. He managed to stay on his feet, however, and grabbing Josh by the hair, flung him with brutal force against the wall.

As Josh struck it, then slid to the floor, dazed, Sutter pulled out his six-gun, his eyes wild. Cocking the gun, he aimed at the nearly unconscious boy. There was no doubt he was about to pull the trigger.

From the floor, Sally screamed, "No! Don't!"

Jenny rushed Sutter. Mary Lou caught her and flung her against the kitchen sink, then drew her own six-gun.

At that moment the doorway went dark and Lone Bear strode swiftly into the kitchen. His smoldering eyes took in the situation with one glance and he started for Sutter, whose back was to him.

"Carl!" Mary Lou warned.

Sutter swung around, saw the big Indian, and pulled his gun off Josh to aim it point-blank at Lone Bear.

"Hold it right there, redskin!" Sutter told him. "One more step and I'll fire."

Lone Bear did not halt. "Fire, white man!"

As the Indian reached out for him, Sutter fired. The big Indian bucked slightly, but with a powerful downward swipe, slapped the gun out of Sutter's hand, then took Sutter's neck in his powerful hands. Crying out in sheer terror, Sutter pulled free, slipped aside and bolted for the door.

Mary Lou cocked her gun and was about to drill Lone Bear in the back when Sally, on her feet now, grabbed a cast-iron frying pan and brought it down as hard as she could on the girl's head. Mary Lou's knees splayed. A second time Sally brought the frying pan down. Mary Lou dropped her weapon and crumpled to the floor.

Jenny snatched up Sutter's revolver and raced out of the kitchen. Sutter had not yet reached his horse. Lifting the revolver, she held it with both hands and fired. The huge weapon bucked wildly upward. The ground beside Sutter exploded. Before she could pull back the hammer and fire a second time, Sutter was on his horse, lashing it toward the cottonwoods. Just to make sure he kept going, she cocked the hammer, aimed at the fleeing rider, closed her eyes, and fired. Without slowing, Sutter reached the trees and splashed through the shallow water to the far side.

Aware for the first time that she was panting like a wild woman, Jenny lowered the heavy revolver. She was trembling from head to foot. Then she thought of Josh and the wounded Lone Bear and rushed back inside.

The tracks leading from the dead horse were not difficult to follow, and by late that same afternoon, Longarm and Billings saw ahead of them a line of cottonwoods and willows. As they neared the stream they glimpsed through the trees the outline of a ranch house and some barns.

"Looks like they're headin' for that ranch on the other side of the stream," Longarm commented.

"Hope not."

"Why?"

"That's the widow's ranch. The Box J."

"A widow? What's her name?"

"Jenny Wills."

"I know her. Met her in Rimrock. She has two children."

"That's her, all right. She's been selling the beef her husband left her to the miners in Mountain City. I don't like the thought of them two outlaws storming her place."

"It's just what they're doing, I'm thinking. They need fresh horses."

"And provisions."

The two men lifted their horses to a lope and, disregarding the tracks, headed straight for the stream. They crossed a shallow ford and pulled up cautiously. Just beyond the cottonwoods, they saw two loaded packhorses standing in the sun, their heads drooping. They looked ready to drop. Closer to the ranch house, a saddle horse was cropping the grass. Its stirrups were set high, Longarm noted at once.

"That horse belongs to the girl," he said. "Where the hell is Sutter's?"

"It could be in the barn," Billings said.

Dismounting, they darted toward the house, guns drawn. They were just skirting the bunkhouse when the kitchen door opened and Sally Henderson burst into the yard and ran toward them.

"You're too late!" she cried. "Sutter's gone."

"What happened?" Longarm asked as he neared her.

"It's all right," she told him excitedly. "We got Mary Lou."

"Whoa there," Billings told her. "Maybe you better slow down some."

Pulling up in front of them, Sally blushed. "I'm sorry," she said. "I'm just so relieved to see you. When you rode in we thought at first you might be more outlaws, or Sutter coming back. Then I recognized Mr. Long, and Jenny recognized you, Sheriff."

"You say Sutter's gone?"

"Yes. Jenny drove him off."

"Drove him off?"

"Lone Bear helped."

"The Ute?"

"Yes, and he's been shot!"

"And the girl," Longarm said, "Mary Lou—you say she's still inside?"

"Yes," Sally replied proudly, her face glowing. "I did it, Mr. Long. I hit her on the head with a frying pan."

"You?" Longarm said, incredulous.

"I knocked her out cold!"

Longarm grinned. "Good for you."

"Come inside! Come inside."

Stepping into the kitchen a moment later behind the sheriff, Longarm saw Mary Lou sitting in a kitchen chair, bound hand and foot. Standing alertly beside her was the boy, Josh, a black cast-iron skillet in his hand. From the look in his eye, Longarm was certain the young towhead would use it if he had to.

Mary Lou glanced up at Longarm and then boldly, defiantly at the sheriff, who strode over and glared down at her.

"It was you and Sutter who held up that stage," the sheriff said. "That right?"

"You mean you doubt it, Sheriff?"

"You also killed the driver and the shotgun messenger."

"I didn't do that."

"They're dead."

"It was Sutter killed them. That marshal standing beside you will testify to that."

"That don't make no matter. You'll hang just the same."

"So hang me and be done with it."

Billings turned abruptly to face Longarm. "What's she mean, Long, calling you 'marshal'?"

Longarm took out his wallet and showed Billings his badge. "See for yourself."

Billings took one glance. "You mean you're a lawman—a deputy U.S. marshal?"

"Out of Denver."

"Why the hell didn't you tell me?"

"What's the matter, Billings? You got something against riding with a U.S. marshal?"

"Not if he tells me who he is."

"Seems to me you were doing all right without my badge."

"You want to tell me what you're doing out here?"

"I was on my way to Mountain City when the stage was held up. And I'm still on my way there."

Longarm could see that Billings knew he was not entirely leveling with him, but the sheriff was smart enough to know there was nothing he could do about it—and experienced enough to realize he'd know all he needed to know when the time came.

Mary Lou grinned maliciously up at Longarm. "Sounds like I let out your dirty little secret."

Longarm stepped closer to her. "Where's my watch?"

"And that cute little belly gun?"

"The derringer. Yes."

"In my saddlebags."

Longarm was satisfied. He knew they wouldn't be going anywhere and he could get them later. Jenny Wills appeared in the kitchen doorway looking disheveled and somewhat distraught, not that he blamed her any.

"I know you," she said to Longarm.

"Yes. In Rimrock. I helped Josh load your provisions into the wagon."

"Oh, yes. You're Mr. Long. Sally says you were in the stage too when it was held up."

"I was."

She looked past Longarm at the sheriff. "Sheriff, please come in here. Lone Bear's been shot."

Billings left the kitchen with her, Longarm following. When they reached her bedroom, they found the Indian lying on the coverlet of Jenny's bed. With alert black eyes he watched them enter. His face was pale, his upper torso bare. Just above his left lung there was a hole the size of a quarter. But the wound was clean. On the night table Longarm saw a bowl of antiseptic; the smell of carbolic acid hung heavy in the room. Longarm guessed that Jenny Wills had been cleaning the wound when Longarm and Billings rode up.

Billings obviously knew Lone Bear, just as he had known those Utes he had encountered in the badlands. "Well, now, Lone Bear. How'd you manage to get that hole in your chest?"

The Indian closed his eyes for a moment, then glanced at Jenny. He obviously did not want to talk about it. So Jenny did. She took a deep breath and described Lone Bear's sudden entrance into the kitchen and its dramatic, frightening aftermath. When she had finished, Billings shook his head at the Indian.

"The way I figure it, Lone Bear, you saved Josh's life."

"He certainly did," Jenny seconded, her voice hushed. "It was a very, very brave thing he did."

"This Indian have no choice," Lone Bear said, his gleaming eyes showing little emotion. "The white outlaw was crazy to shoot the boy."

"Sheriff," Jenny said, her voice urgent, "can you take Lone Bear back with you to Rimrock?"

"Why?"

"Can't you see? He needs a doctor. I've done all I can."

"Sorry, Miss Jenny, we're going on to Mountain City, not back to Rimrock. From the looks of things, we got ourselves some gold to deliver to the Wells Fargo Express office. And we got to take that little girl gunslick to the lockup. Then we still got Carl Sutter to track down. He shot down the stage driver and the shotgun in cold blood."

"I understand that. But what of Lone Bear?"

"Look, Miss Jenny, if Lone Bear shows up wounded in Rimrock, someone's bound to wire the army, tell them there's an uprising, that not all the Utes are on their reservation where they rightfully belong."

"Now, Sheriff, really. Everyone knows there are plenty of Utes still around here."

"Everyone knows, Miss Jenny, but no one sees them. They keep in the badlands and stay pretty well hid. And if they're smart, they'll keep it that way."

Jenny sighed. "All right," she said. "I'll do what I can for Lone Bear myself then."

"I ain't worried none," Billings said comfortingly.

"I'm sure you'll pull him through all right. Besides, he's one tough old buffalo."

Billings winked at Lone Bear. The impassive Indian did not wink back, but he did seem genuinely pleased at the sheriff's words.

Less than an hour later, Jenny stood in the doorway with Josh and Annie and waved good-bye to her new friend Sally Henderson, who was riding out with the sheriff and the U.S. deputy marshal. She was once more on her way to meet that school committee in Mountain City. Jenny hoped that in the years to come, she would visit. But she realized how unlikely that would be. This valley was a long way from Mountain City, and a woman as pretty as Sally would soon find a multitude of distractions.

Before she passed from sight, Sally turned in her saddle and waved one final good-bye.

Jenny lifted her arm. "Wave good-bye, children."

They did so, and kept waving until the caravan of horsemen and packhorses passed out of sight beyond the trees. Jenny turned back into the house, walked down the hall into the kitchen and sat wearily down at the table. She felt a yawning emptiness. In that short while she had come to like Sally Henderson very much, and now here she was alone again, and this time with a very badly wounded man on her hands.

She was doing all she could to help Lone Bear, but she could not be sure it was the right thing, or that it was doing him any good. All she knew for sure was that the bullet was still in Lone Bear's chest, and that she had no idea how she was going to get it out. She could tell nothing from Lone Bear's reaction. No matter how deeply she had poked into that terrible wound in his chest, he had not uttered a sound.

He was a very stoical—and remarkable—man.

But she was not a remarkable woman. And right now that was what Lone Bear needed.

"Look, Ma," said Josh. He was standing in the kitchen's open door.

Jenny got up from the table and looked past Josh. An Indian rider was approaching from the south. As he got closer, Jenny saw that he was a squat, older Ute with long white hair that fell past his shoulders like a girl's.

She felt an enormous weariness fall over her. This was just what she needed at this point, a hungry Indian to feed.

"Stay here," she told the children. "I will greet this old man and see what he wants."

She walked out into the yard and waited for the Indian to reach her. When he did, he halted his pony and looked impassively down at her. "I am Eagle Claw," he said. "I bring medicine for Lone Bear."

Jenny was astonished. How in the world had this Indian found out about Lone Bear's terrible wound? But it mattered little how he had found it out. He was here and would surely help.

"Thank you for coming," she said eagerly. "Lone Bear is in my house. I will take you to him."

The Indian slid off his horse, lifted a colorful medicine bag from around his pony's neck, and followed Jenny to the ranch house. Both of them solemn and wide-eyed, Josh and Annie watched the old Indian approach the house and enter the kitchen.

"Lone Bear is in my bedroom," Jenny said, pointing the way. Without a word, the Indian marched down the hall and disappeared into her bedroom. Silencing the children with a finger to her lips, Jenny left them in the kitchen and followed after the old Indian.

Eagle Claw was already bent over Lone Bear, and Lone Bear already seemed to be much better. Color had flowed back into his face. It seemed obvious to Jenny that it was the presence of Eagle Claw alone that gave him heart. He obviously had great confidence in the medicine man's healing art.

Jenny watched as Eagle Claw inspected Lone Bear's wound, then swiftly opened his bag and took out his salves and potions and finally a long, forcepslike bone instrument. This, she realized, was what the medicine man would use to extract the bullet. At once she was certain that Lone Bear was going to survive. She could feel it in every fiber of her being. There was strength in him that no single bullet could extinguish.

In that instant, Jenny realized that to be Lone Bear's squaw would be one thing, but to be his wife would be something else again. Lone Bear looked up at Jenny and smiled—and in that smile Jenny saw all his love and trust. She went to the side of the bed and took his hand in hers. As they gazed at each other, she knew they had come to an understanding.

Her eyes misted over with happiness.

Chapter 10

Two days later, close to ten in the evening, Longarm and Billings rode into Mountain City. From the unnatural quiet of the place, it was obvious the miners were still on strike. The narrow streets, hemmed in between vaulting mountain walls, were nearly deserted. From within the saloons they rode past, tinkling pianos echoed; the gambling halls were close to empty. Bar girls and some parlor-house women—rouged and dressed in bright tinsel and black stockings—were clustered on the porches. Some waved hopefully at Longarm and Billings as they rode past. They looked unmussed and were restless for employment. Without the pockets of free-spending miners to empty, they were enjoying an extended holiday, probably the first one they had known in a long time.

Billings slowed when they neared the hotel and checked his mount until he was riding alongside Longarm. He had said little since they left the Wills ranch. Glancing coldly at Longarm, he suggested Longarm deliver Mary Lou to his two deputies at the jailhouse a block farther on, while he brought the gold on farther to the Wells Fargo Express office.

"What about me?" Sally asked wearily as she halted her mount alongside Longarm. "I don't have any idea where I can find the school-board members at this hour."

"I figured you could take a room at this hotel," Longarm suggested, "until those school-board members show up."

Sally blushed. "I'm penniless, Longarm. I lost everything in the stage holdup. I can't afford a room."

He laughed gently. "Sure you can. I'll be back later to take care of it."

"You?"

"That's right."

"But what'll I tell the desk clerk?"

"Tell him to see to your horse, then explain to him that your brother will be along shortly to get a room of his own."

She was obviously grateful, but too weary to show it. As Longarm and Billings rode on up the street, she turned her horse and urged it toward the hotel's hitch rail. A few minutes later, as Longarm neared the jailhouse, Billings turned in his saddle and handed Longarm the reins to Mary Lou's horse, then took from him the reins of the packhorses he had been leading.

"Them two I deputized are Tim Hoskins and Dale Rogers," Billings told him. "Tell 'em I'll be back soon's I deliver this here gold." His contemptuous glance took in Mary Lou, who was riding slumped over the pommel, her wrists bound to the saddle horn with a strip of horsehide. He looked back at Longarm. "And tell them to keep their hands off this here scorpion. She's still got plenty of venom left in her. I suggest you deal with Tim Hoskins. He's the oldest one, and the least foolish."

The sheriff continued on alone, the three weary packhorses following behind, their heads down, their tails drooping. Longarm nudged his horse toward the hitch rail in front of the jailhouse and dismounted. As he untied Mary Lou from the saddle horn, she stirred sullenly and glared down at him.

"We here?"

"We're here."

He reached up and pulled Mary Lou out of the saddle. When she landed beside him, she pulled away suddenly and lashed out with a foot, the tip of her boot catching Longarm smartly on a shin. He slapped her smartly, turning her head almost completely around.

"You bastard!" she cried, staggering back. "You'd hit a lady!"

"No, not a lady. But I would hit you."

He turned her roughly, and with one hand on her collar, the other on her tiny buttocks, ran her up the porch steps and into the jailhouse office. The deputy at the desk jumped up. The other one was asleep on the cot with his mouth open. He remained asleep despite the clamor.

"Who are you, mister?" the deputy demanded, pushing his chair back and circling the desk. The older of the two, it must be Hoskins, Longarm realized. Sandy-haired, lean, with a leathery face and cool blue eyes, he looked decidedly tougher than his sidekick.

"Name's Custis Long," Longarm replied.

"And who in hell you got there?"

"She's a gift from Sheriff Billings," Longarm told him laconically. "This here's Mary Lou. It was her and two others who held up the Mountain City stage a few days back."

Hoskins took a more careful look at the sullen girl. "Sheriff Billings, you say? Where is he?"

"On his way to the Wells Fargo office with the gold they took."

The other deputy was awake now. Scratching his head, he sat up on the edge of the cot, blinking sleepily first at Mary Lou, then at Longarm.

"Gold, you say?"

"You heard me."

Mary Lou squirmed free suddenly and made a grab for the derringer Longarm had rescued from her saddlebag. She managed to get her fingers around the gold chain before Longarm sent her reeling backward into Hoskins's arms.

Dale Rogers jumped to his feet. "Hey, mister, you just hit a woman!"

"He'll hit you, if you don't shut up," Hoskins told him as he grabbed Mary Lou.

Longarm stepped quickly forward and took back his watch and derringer from the smoldering girl, not an easy task, since he was forced to peel her fingers from around the chain one at a time.

When he finished, she spat on him.

"You son of a bitch," she snarled.

Longarm turned and strode toward the door. As he reached it, he looked back at Deputy Hoskins. "Billings told me to warn you. But maybe I don't need to. Anyway, he said she's still got plenty of venom left. I suggest you two keep your distance."

As he opened the door, he glanced back. Mary Lou, hissing and twisting like a wild cat, was trying to squirm out of Hoskins's grasp as the other deputy hurried over to unlock a cell door. Not until he saw the door slam shut on her did he descend the steps. Mounting up, he rode back down the main street, heading for the livery stable across from the hotel.

As Longarm approached the front desk, the balding clerk put on a greasy smile and nudged his wire-rimmed spectacles up onto his nose.

"I'd like a room for the night," Longarm told him. "My sister already registered. I'll pay for her room, too."

"Ah, then you must be Mr. Henderson."

"Wrong. Name's Custis Long."

Longarm turned the register around and signed it. In some confusion, the desk clerk handed him his room key.

"What room did you give my sister?" Longarm asked.

"Er . . . number twelve."

Longarm looked at his key. He had eleven, the room next to hers. He mounted the steps to the second floor. On the way to his room, he paused before Sally's door and rapped softly.

"Yes . . . ?" Sally's voice was fogged with sleep.

"Sorry to wake you, Sally," he said. "I'm in the next room if you need anything. Good night."

"Good night, Custis," she replied sleepily.

Longarm continued on to his room, peeled out of his

135

clothes, and was soon asleep himself. Sometime around midnight, however, he came awake, every sense alert.

At first he could not be sure what had awakened him. Then he heard the sound of a crowd surging through the street below his window. He tried to ignore the disturbance and get back to sleep, but found it impossible. Flipping back his sheets, he padded barefoot to the window. The mountain night was cool and before going to bed, Longarm had closed the window. He flung it open and leaned out.

The narrow street and sidewalks were crowded with miners. When he caught some of what they were shouting, he understood at once what was afoot. Someone had let it be known that the newly minted gold had finally been delivered to the Wells Fargo Express office. These miners, despite the lateness of the hour, wanted their pay.

They had waited long enough.

The mine owners, it appeared, had already been sent for and were now on their way to the Wells Fargo office to distribute the men's pay. The miners were jubilant. They would soon have hard currency jingling in their pockets. A holiday atmosphere prevailed, and Longarm had no doubt that before long the saloons, parlor houses, and gambling halls would be running wide open, and would stay open through to dawn and well into the next day. The strike was over.

Someone rapped tentatively on his door.

"Who is it?" he called.

"Sally."

"Just a minute."

Longarm pulled on his pants, ran his hands quickly through his thick hair, and opened the door.

"I hear shouting in the streets," Sally said. "It awakened me."

"Come in. It woke me up too."

She stepped in hesitantly. The nightgown Jenny Wills had given her was not quite long enough to cover her ankles and the slippers she was wearing were a size too large. She had combed out her hair and the long tresses gleamed darkly in the unlighted room. Longarm closed the door and led her over to the window so she could look down at the crowd.

"What's going on?" Sally asked, her voice hushed.

"They heard about the gold getting here. It looks like they're not going to wait until tomorrow for the mine owners to distribute the wages due them."

"At this ungodly hour?"

"I figure the owners are just as happy to pay them now. The strike will be over that much sooner."

Overcome with exuberance, a miner took out his side arm and began firing into the air. The idea caught on rapidly and soon the night was exploding like a Chinese New Year. Startled, Sally pulled back from the window. Longarm closed the window and slumped into a motheaten armchair beside the bed.

"Looks like we're not going to get much sleep tonight."

She shook her head and sat wearily down on the edge of his bed. "It's all so unreal, so strange. I keep wondering when all this madness is going to fade away and all I'll have to worry about is my class full of young scholars."

"Soon as you find those school-board members."

"Yes." She sighed. "But perhaps they have long since given up on me."

137

"Don't worry. We'll scare them up again. I'll hang around until you get hold of them."

She looked at him for a long moment, studying him. Then she said, "You're very kind."

Longarm said nothing. Whenever a woman said anything like that to him, he had found over the years, his best response was silence. It would usually not be long before the woman decided she knew just how to thank him for his kindness. He hated to think Sally was as easy to read as this, but she was not all that different from any other woman.

Before long, she reached out to him.

He left the armchair and sat close beside her on the bed. She leaned her head against his chest, sighing. He draped one arm about her shoulder and began stroking her hair.

She snuggled closer. "Only this," she told him softly, "is real. Everything else is unreal, an ugly nightmare."

She was wrong, of course. Everything that had happened to her was real. Only too real. But if it made her feel any better to believe what she did, who was he to set her straight? As he continued to stroke her hair, she turned her head to look up at him.

"Aren't you going to kiss me?"

"Is that what you want?"

"Do I have to beg?"

"It's not that, Sally. I just figured after all you'd been through, you wouldn't want me to . . ."

"My God, Custis," she exclaimed, her deep laugh suddenly filling the room. "Wouldn't *want* you to? Why in the world not? I've been bullied by my fiancé and cast aside. I've come more than halfway across this continent, only to lose all I own in a stagecoach robbery

...been chased off a cliff in a thunderstorm by an odious fat man...carried through the rain by an Indian whose stonelike silence terrified me. Yes, I'm in the mood, Custis. In the mood for someone real and good to hold me close and tell me the ugliness is behind me. God, Custis, my luck *has* to change, and I want you to change it."

"But I assumed...I mean you're not a..."

Again she laughed. "A virgin, Custis? You mean you don't want to be the one to deflower me?"

"I guess that's about the most delicate way to put it."

"How gallant of you, Custis. But you need not worry. I have not lived this long without knowing a man. Fortunately, it was not my fiancé who initiated me. But I have had my few stolen moments, most of the time with callow young men who were more eager than expert. Perhaps I was a bit wild, Custis, but at this moment, I just don't give a damn. And neither should you."

Lifting her face to his, she placed a hand against the back of his head and gently drew his lips down onto hers. Her mouth opened hungrily and soon he was lost in the hot, wet fire of her kiss. It was definitely *not* the kiss of a virgin and it warmed him like good whiskey.

Her lips released his at last and she looked deep into his eyes. "Do with me what you will, Longarm."

"Please?"

"Yes, damn you. Please."

Swiftly unbuttoning the front of her nightgown, she flung it aside, revealing her incredibly ripe fullness. Longarm wasted no time peeling out of his britches, and in a moment their long naked bodies were entwined. Lifting onto his elbows, he prowled hungrily atop her, taking in all of her, especially the wonder of her dark hair coiling about her marvelous upthrust breasts.

Impatient, she reached up and held his cheeks between her palms and kissed him again, her tongue probing deeply, and he wondered where in hell this Boston schoolmarm had learned such tricks. He felt her writhing slowly, lasciviously under him as her hips parted hungrily to facilitate him.

Wishing to prolong it, Longarm brought his hand up to cup one of her silken breasts. His rough fingertips caressed the nipple. He heard her deep-throated groan, and felt her arms tightening about his neck while she surged under him, thrusting her muff up against his erection. His head spun drunkenly with his need for her. He could smell her, the scent of a woman fully aroused, a thousand times more exciting than any perfume. But still he held back, and bending his head to her breast, took a nipple in his mouth, causing it to swell and become as hard as a bullet as he flicked it expertly with his tongue. Sally groaned and reached down for his crotch. Grabbing him fiercely, she opened her thighs still wider.

He could deny neither her nor himself any longer. He placed his big hand under her buttocks, lifted her, then plunged in past her hot moist entrance. It was like coming home after a long ride in unfriendly country.

For both of them.

"Ah!" she cried, flinging her head back.

Bringing up her legs, she locked her ankles around the back of his neck, and again he wondered where in the hell she had learned that trick. But only for a moment as he ground eagerly down into her.

"Deeper, Custis!" she commanded huskily.

Longarm did his best to comply. Pulling almost completely out of her, he kept his tip just inside her, then plunged back down into her. He felt himself striking the very depths of her. She uttered a sharp, guttural cry. Her ankles tightened convulsively about his neck as she leaned back to take him, all of him. Perfectly willing to comply, he drove into her again and again, going deeper, it seemed, with each powerful thrust.

"Yes, yes, yes," she muttered through clenched teeth, flinging her head back and forth wildly. "Oh, yes, that's it, Custis! Don't stop now!"

Longarm had no such intention. Smiling grimly, he increased his pace and the depth of his thrusts, driving her up against the headboard. She shuddered and began hammering him furiously about the head and shoulders with clenched fists. Hunching against her wild attack, he continued to drive until at last, crying out intensely, she climaxed.

He was about to pull out, but she was not finished. She clung to him still, shuddering in a series of climaxes. Her cry became a wail, and as she continued to erupt, he felt himself losing control as well—until he could hold back no longer and plunged over the edge, hammering down upon her, exploding inside her, expending his full quota of seed.

He lifted off her. Her face was shiny with perspiration.

"You see," she said, smiling radiantly up at him. "I am not a virgin, Custis."

"No, you are not."

"But the men of Boston know only how to please themselves, I am afraid. That was the first time I experienced what a woman properly eased is supposed to feel. I see now what all the fuss is about."

He lay down on the bed beside her. She drew her long, silken thighs against him again and thrust hungrily. It was clear she wanted more, and before long, he realized he did, too.

"Your education has just begun," he told her.

"What do you mean?"

"Get on top of me."

"You mean . . . ?"

"Yes."

"But . . . won't that hurt?"

"Just go easy. You'll soon get the hang of it."

She slipped astride him and with his help, guided herself back down onto him. She sighed at last and leaned back, prolonging the pleasure of it as much as she could. He told her to rotate slightly. She did so and at once found the pleasure of it. He leaned back and let her long hair stream down her back.

As she bounced more and more energetically on his pole he held himself back, concerned only with her pleasure. Now, however, he could wait no longer. With indecent haste, he rolled her over, and mounted her. He was as hot as a five-dollar pistol.

"So soon, Custis?" she gasped up at him. "Can you manage it?"

"Don't you worry about me none, Sally," he told her. "Just lay back and enjoy it."

"Just as you say, Custis."

He was already thrusting with quick, savage strokes —no longer holding back, no longer concerned with her climax. Soon, she too was caught up in the intensity of his need and before long was meeting him thrust for thrust, her inner muscles holding his erection like a warm, lubricious hand. Grateful, he pounded on with fast, repeated, driving thrusts that slammed her repeatedly into the bed. Her startled cries gave way to pleased grunts and her body began to pulse in perfect tune with his. Once their wild thrusting meshed, the savage intensity of their lovemaking increased in a building, syncopated rhythm as she drew him still deeper into her muff. Arching her back, a series of wild sobs broke from her.

Longarm pounded on mindlessly. A cry escaped his own lips and then—for the second time that night—he was hurtling over the edge, pouring his seed once more into her.

Gasping, he dropped forward onto her, his face resting in the cleft of her incandescent breasts. He was spent utterly, and he could tell Sally was also. When their breathing had quieted some, Sally ran her fingers through his sweaty hair and murmured happily, blissfully.

"Thanks for the lesson, Custis."

"You're a fast learner."

"I'll accept that as a compliment."

He eased off her and propped his head up on his elbow as he gazed at her body. It gleamed softly from head to foot with tiny beads of perspiration. The musky, not unpleasant smell of their lovemaking filled the room. "That's how I meant it, Sally. As a compliment. You're a lot of woman."

"And you're a lot of man. I had to come quite a ways, it seems, to find one. And right now, I'm glad I did."

The uproar in the street below had subsided some. Longarm got up and padded on bare feet over to the window and looked down. Miners were streaming back from the direction of the express office and pouring into the saloons and gambling halls. The girls who had been congregating on the porches were out of sight now, presumably inside the saloons and parlor houses plying their trades. As Longarm had surmised, the miners were going to make a night of it, and the saloons and parlor houses seemed more than willing to oblige, no matter the hour.

He returned to the bed and sat on its edge, idly scratching his long naked shanks. "Looks like by tomorrow this town will be back to normal. Fact is it might be real quiet for a while."

"You mean while they sleep off tonight."

Longarm nodded, drinking in the sight of her lush body. Enough light was filtering in through the windows so he didn't have to light the table lamp, and that he did not want to do. A lamp's harsh, unforgiving glare would spoil this quiet, delicious moment.

"What town did you say this school was in?" he asked her.

"I didn't. I just assumed it was outside of Mountain City."

"Why?"

"What on earth would miners want with a school?"

"Before they discovered the copper in an abandoned mine and found a way to extract it from the tailings, from what I heard, this town was becoming a quiet enough place, the gold and silver mines settling into a slow but steady production. Billings told me it was the copper that unsettled things, turned the town into another bonanza. But that'll pass. The veins'll peter out, things'll settle down again and soon enough there'll be women and children—and schools."

"You mean I might end up teaching here?"

He grinned at her. "You might at that."

She shuddered.

"It won't be so bad."

"I hope you're right." She said nothing for a few moments, then looked questioningly at him. "Custis, what are you going to do now?"

"Go after Sutter."

"Isn't that the sheriff's job?"

"I suppose it is. But he won't mind if I tag along."

"Are you sure of that?"

"Why do you ask?"

"He seems very cool to you. Wary. Did something happen between you two?"

"A little while back he found out I was a deputy U.S. marshal."

"Why would that upset him?"

Longarm avoided Sally's penetrating gaze. "I don't know why—unless he has something to hide."

"Sheriff Billings?"

He looked at her. "There's something you ought to remember, Sally. If you're going to live out here, that is. Few westerners were born here, unless they're Indians. That means everyone you meet has a past. So as far as you're concerned, it's always best to simply assume they were all born yesterday."

"What you mean is that Sheriff Billings has a past."

"Just like the rest of us."

"Does that include you?"

He smiled at her and shrugged.

"And what about me?"

"You have one. Now. But no one's going to pry, and neither should you."

"You're a fine southern gentleman, Custis Long."

145

"Thank you, ma'am."

"But you must tell me. If the sheriff has a past, does that mean he's the one you're after? Or is it really Sutter you want?"

Maybe both, Longarm reminded himself. But he had no intention of admitting this to her. "It's Carl Sutter I'm after, Sally. He's a wanted man. This isn't the first stagecoach he's robbed, and if we don't haul him in, it won't be the last."

She thought that over, obviously accepting his answer. "He's such a terrible man. Just the thought of him makes me shudder."

"He's bad news, all right."

"Now. Get back down here beside me," she said abruptly. "I need you to keep me warm."

"Have mercy, woman. I'm all spent."

She laughed devilishly. "Then we'll just cuddle."

Not a bad idea, Longarm realized, as he slipped down beside her and lifted a sheet over them. The sound coming from the street below their window gradually faded, or they fell asleep.

It didn't really matter which.

Chapter 11

Early the next morning Longarm got a shave, a haircut, and a bath. Afterward, striding from the barbershop on the lookout for a restaurant, he saw Billings crossing the street toward him. Longarm pulled up and waited for the sheriff to reach him.

"Been looking for you, Long. Want to talk to you."

"Not here. Why not join me for breakfast?"

"Already had mine. But I'll join you anyway. I could use another coffee. There's a good restaurant down the street."

"Suits me."

Inside the restaurant, they found a table along a wall in the back. Longarm ordered, then waited for Billings to speak up. It was obvious the man had been waiting a long time for this chance. And Longarm had a pretty good idea what was on the man's mind.

"What are your plans, Long?"

"Sutter."

"I can handle him."

"I don't doubt that."

"So you don't need to come along."

"Why don't you let me be the judge of that?"

"Is Carl Sutter the reason you were on that stage?"

"I told you why I was on that stage. I suspected it was going to be held up."

"I don't think you're answering my question."

"Sutter's a wanted man, Billings. Back in Denver, we've got dodgers aplenty on the son of a bitch. That's how I was able to recognize him in Rimrock."

"Hell, man. You had no idea Sutter was going to turn up in Rimrock. That was pure, blind chance."

"So? What does that prove?"

"That it's me you're after."

"That so?"

"That's what I think."

"Would you want to tell me why I would be after you, Sheriff?"

"It's a feeling I got."

Longarm took a deep, troubled breath. He had no more stomach for this evasion. Billings deserved a straight answer. He was too good a man to be hazed like this.

"All right, Billings. I'll level with you. Seems we got a friend in common."

"Yeah? Who might that be?"

"Billy Vail."

"Vail? Billy Vail? You know him?"

"Billy Vail is the U.S. marshal in Denver. He's my boss. He's the one sent me looking for you."

"Billy Vail's a U.S. marshal?" Billings's astonishment gave way to a slow, pleased smile. It was clear he still thought highly of his old trail buddy.

"Yep. He runs the First District Court in Colorado."

"Jesus," Billings said softly, shaking his head. "That old son of a bitch."

Longarm's breakfast arrived. Longarm began to eat while the sheriff leaned back, sipping his coffee and gazing out the window, his eyes distant. It was Longarm's feeling that Billings might be thinking of his old buddy again, riding through old towns, tearing up saloons, chasing bandidos.

And chasing other things too.

Good manners dictated that Billings wait until Longarm cleaned his plate before resuming the conversation. When Longarm finished up finally and reached for his coffee, Billings spoke up.

"So it's Billy sent you after me, is it? Why?"

"That heist in North Dakota."

Billings sighed and shook his head wearily. "That's what I figured."

"You admitting you were a member of that gang?"

"I am."

"Then I'll have to take you in."

"I figured that, too. But I want Sutter first. He killed a man I knew and liked."

"The stage driver?"

"That's right."

Longarm considered for only a moment before nodding his agreement. "Sure. Go after Sutter. Just so long as I go with you."

"Don't see how I could stop that, Long."

"You got any idea on how to find the bastard?"

"I have. It's kind of tricky, though."

149

"I'm listening."

"I already been in the lockup to see that witch we brought in. When I asked her to tell me where Sutter had gone, she spat through the bars at me."

"Sounds like her, all right."

"I told her we didn't need her and she let loose with some well-chosen words that made the young deputy blush, and then blurted out that we'd never find Sutter, not where he'd gone. She said we'd never find him in a million years."

Longarm finished his coffee. "Now what?"

"Don't you get it? She as good as said she knows where Sutter's holed up."

"Makes sense she'd know that. But it's not likely she's going to tell you where Sutter is."

"You don't have much imagination, Long. All we have to do is let her loose and then follow her."

"Risky, isn't it?"

"If I want Sutter, it's my best bet. I could spend a year searching through these mountains. And I don't figure you got that much patience, either."

"I figure you've got a plan. So what is it?"

"I've already spoken to Tim Hoskins and the kid, Rogers. Tonight they'll get very drunk, so drunk they'll pass out and leave that witch's cell door unlocked. There'll be a gun within easy reach."

"Hey..."

"Don't get in no lather, Marshal. It'll be filled with blanks. I'm not crazy."

"Tonight, you say."

"Yes. Late."

"Can you trust those two deputies to handle this?"

"I ain't so sure of the kid. But Hoskins knows his way around. He can handle it."

Longarm considered a moment, then nodded briskly. "Then I say we do it."

Billings finished his coffee and got to his feet. "By the way, when I went looking for you just now, I saw Sally Henderson in the hotel lobby with a tall gent and three other men. Looks like she found that school committee wants to hire her."

"That's good to know," Longarm said, fishing in his pants pocket for money to pay his check. "Where'll I meet you tonight?"

"In the hotel lobby. Around eleven."

Entering the hotel a few minutes later, Longarm saw no sign of Sally in the lobby and went upstairs and knocked softly on her door. Sally opened the door promptly. She was dressed in one of the outfits Jenny Wills had given her. It was a tight fit, but she still looked pretty damn nice. And maybe that was because of the tight fit.

"Custis!" she cried, drawing him into her room. "I've been looking all over for you!"

"Well, here I am."

"I have wonderful news. I have just met the school board. They're sending a carriage around to take me to the school! It should be here any minute."

"That *is* good news."

"They just built the school, and there's a small apartment in back for me. I'm sure it will work out just fine. And Custis, they're paying me fifty dollars a month!"

"Sounds wonderful, Sally."

A knock sounded on the open door behind Longarm. He turned to see a tall, handsome gent striding into the room, his flat-brimmed Stetson in his hand. He was dressed in an expensive gray suit and wore a starched collar and string tie. But he was no dandy. His weather-beaten face and sharp, clear brown eyes testified to that.

"Custis," Sally said, "this gentleman is Nelson Miles, the head of the Mountain City Board of Education. He's an engineer at one of the mines."

"The Potluck," Miles told Longarm, smiling and extending his hand.

Longarm shook the offered hand and found it tough as leather, the grip solid.

"I'm pleased to meet you, Mr. Long," Miles said. "You have no idea how worried we were about Miss Henderson when the stage failed to show up and we learned what had happened."

"I can imagine."

"It's been a long wait, Mr. Long. But the result has been worth it." As he said this, he smiled almost shyly at Sally. "The members of the board are most grateful to you. Miss Henderson has already told us how you and Sheriff Billings saved her from the outlaws who robbed the stage."

"It was a Ute Indian who helped the most."

"Yes. Of course. She told us about the Indian." He turned to Sally then, unable to hide the pleasure he felt gazing upon her. "I've brought the carriage around, Miss Henderson. As soon as you're ready, we can ride out to see the school."

"Oh, I'm ready right now."

She had already tied her hair up into a bun. Snatching the hat Jenny had provided off her bed, she put it on carefully, then flung her arms exuberantly around Longarm's neck and pecked him on the cheek.

"I'm checking out of the hotel now," she told him. "Mr. Miles has graciously paid for my room, and I'll spend the afternoon settling into my apartment."

"So this is good-bye."

"Yes, but surely you'll come to see me before you leave Mountain City?"

"You'll be very busy. And so will I. Good-bye and good luck, Sally. You've come a long way, and it hasn't been easy for you—but I don't think you're going to regret it."

"I'll personally see to that, Mr. Long," Miles quickly assured him.

Longarm looked at him. "You be sure and do that."

As Sally hurried out the door with Miles, she glanced quickly back at Longarm. "And thank you, Custis," she said, smiling, "for everything."

He waved and followed her out of the hotel room. Closing the door behind him, he watched Sally vanish down the stairs on Nelson Miles's arm—a man who was obviously not going to waste the opportunity fate had thrown his way. If Longarm was any judge of the look in a smitten man's eye, Sally Henderson had found more than a teaching position here in Mountain City.

Longarm crouched down in the alley across from the jailhouse. Mountain City was quiet tonight. The miners had exhausted themselves completely the night before and had not entirely recovered yet. Besides, most of them were broke once again. Farther back in the alley behind him, Longarm's saddled mount waited. Billings was waiting behind the jailhouse. Now all that was required was for Mary Lou to play her part.

A few minutes ago the two deputies, staggering convincingly, had entered the jailhouse. At the hitch rail in front of it, a saddled mount swished its tail. There was a rifle in the boot, its firing pin filed down. They weren't being nice to trick Mary Lou in this fashion, but Mary Lou was not a nice person.

A Colt detonated inside the office and Longarm heard a man cry out. It was, he trusted, a part of Tim Hoskins's act. The door burst open. Mary Lou, her hat on, the big gun they had left for her in her hand, swept down the steps, caught up the reins of the waiting horse, and swung aboard. Longarm stepped out of the alley's mouth and watched her gallop down the street and out of town. A few townsmen ran out into the street, drawn by the sound of gunfire. Others followed after them and soon a crowd was surging toward the jailhouse to investigate the gunshots.

As soon as Longarm saw the two deputies standing in the open jailhouse doorway, he swung onto his mount and galloped out of the alley after Mary Lou. Once clear of Mountain City, he could hear the clatter of Billings's horse behind him and reined in to let the sheriff overtake him.

Pulling up beside him, Billings glanced at the night sky. "Damn," he said, "there's not much of a moon tonight."

"She's just ahead of us," Longarm told him. "I figure she'll keep to this trail."

"It's the only one out of this valley."

Billings clapped spurs to his mount and swept into the night ahead of Longarm. Longarm followed and they soon found themselves riding southwest, toward the pass that led out of the valley. Day came and they were still on her trail, even though they could no longer hear the rap of her mount's hoofs. When they came to a creek where Mary Lou had stopped, they took the opportunity to halt also to take care of their mounts and fill their canteens. Before they mounted up again, Billings walked over and pointed to the fresh tracks Mary Lou's mount had left in the soft ground beside the stream.

Longarm bent to peer more closely at them and saw that Billings had had the foresight to notch the left front shoe. It stood out as clearly as a sign post. Longarm was impressed. Billings was no fool.

They mounted up and kept on after Mary Lou. So far, Longarm realized, things were going nicely. Mary Lou could have taken other trails that would have been considerably more difficult for them to follow, but she hadn't. She had taken the bait and was running flat out. When it came time to reel her back in, they would be on Sutter's doorstep.

Or so they hoped.

For three days they followed her tracks, being careful never to top a rise that might give her a glimpse of them. During those days they never attempted to get close enough to see her, content to follow her tracks deeper and still deeper into the mountains. On one occasion they held their breath as she skirted a small horse ranch, for if she decided to look in on it to do some looting of her own, they would have had to ride down on her and halt the operation.

But Billings had thought of this, too. He explained to Longarm that he had tied a bedroll to her cantle and had loaded her two saddlebgs with hardtack, canned beans, salt pork, and other provisions, thus assuring that Mary Lou would have no need to rob any lone rancher for food.

Throughout the third day, Mary Lou led them through a series of torturous, labyrinthine canyons that cut back on themselves in a confusing and seemingly impenetrable badlands that took them through steep-sided arroyos and across ice-cold, snow-melt streams. At times her tracks led them through gorges so narrow the two men had to ride through in single file.

By mid-afternoon of the fourth day, they put this tortured land behind them and close to sundown rode out of a patch of timber to find themselves gazing down at a lushly carpeted, stream-fed valley. On the other side of the valley, the dim outline of a cabin could be glimpsed set back against a towering rock face. A long, shale-littered slope led up to the cabin, giving anyone inside a pretty good look at whoever might be riding up that slope for a visit.

At that moment the rider was Mary Lou.

Longarm and Billings turned their horses back into the timber's cover and dismounted.

"Hot damn!" Billings cried. "We got him now."

"Looks like it," said Longarm, snaking a Winchester out of his saddle boot. "We never would have found this place without her."

"We'll wait until night," Billings said. "There's no way we can make it up that slope undetected in this light."

"It won't be much easier tonight," Longarm reminded him.

Billings had been in the act of tying his mount to a sapling. He swung about to face Longarm. "Hell, Marshal. I don't need you for this. You can ride back out of here anytime you want."

Longarm just smiled and shook his head. "You can't get rid of me that easy, Sheriff."

"No," Billings acknowledged ruefully. "Guess maybe I can't."

Billings smiled then, but it gave neither man warmth. Longarm understood the sheriff's dilemma perfectly. At the moment he was not only the hunter, but the hunted. Though Longarm wished things could be different, he didn't see how he could change the situation any and stay on the level with Billy Vail.

And himself.

The door was pulled open suddenly and Carl grabbed Mary Lou's arm and yanked her into the cabin. Slamming the door, he whirled on her.

"Jesus Christ! Where in hell did you come from, Mary Lou?"

"Ain't you glad to see me?"

"Sure, I'm glad to see you. But last I knew you were in that ranch house and someone was beating on your head with a frying pan."

"Sheriff Billings came by with that deputy marshal and took me and the gold to Mountain City. But I broke loose from my cell and lit out."

"Jesus," Carl said, shaking his head. "I never would've believed it! You showin' up like this. Good thing you didn't waste any time. I got my horse all loaded up, ready to pull out tomorrow morning, first thing."

"How much gold you got?" she asked, eyes gleaming.

He grinned back at her. "Don't worry. Enough to set us up for a good long time."

She stepped close and flung her arms around his neck, grinding her crotch into his. "That means we got the night to celebrate."

"Hell, ain't much to celebrate in this place," he told her, pulling his lips away from hers and stepping back. "I ain't got no food left and damn little water. Have to haul it half a mile. I'll be damn glad to get out of here."

"No grub? None at all?"

"I got some coffee left."

She smiled triumphantly. "Then go check the saddlebags on my horse," she told him, "while I get this stove going. I didn't bring no whiskey, but we're going to have ourselves a feast, Carl. To celebrate my finding you. Then we'll go to bed and *really* celebrate."

Carl hurried from the cabin to return a moment later lugging the two saddlebags, a wide grin on his face. As he laid them down on the table, his face darkened momentarily. He glanced at her.

"You sure you weren't followed?"

"You know me better than that, Carl. I watched the trail behind me every morning for half an hour. I never once saw a glint of sunlight on metal nor heard a bit jingle. No one followed me. Hell, Carl, I lit out of that town like a scorched cat. No, sir. No one followed me."

Satisfied, he grinned at her. "Tell me what happened," he said as he dumped the cans of beans and other provisions out onto the table.

"The two deputies guarding me came in as drunk as lords," she told him, poking fresh firewood into the stove's belly. "I asked them to empty out my slops jar. One of them did, but when he came back with it, I noticed he was so drunk, he forgot to lock my cell door. Later when he and his partner fell asleep, I pushed open the door, grabbed his weapon up off his desk. One of the deputies came awake and tried to stop me. I shot him in the gut and lit out. If he dies, I guess I'll be wanted for murder."

"Don't give it a thought, Mary Lou," he said. "Join the club. I lost track of the poor sonsofbitches I put away."

The fire going, she attacked one of the cans of beans with a can opener. Watching her, he said, "That's a nice horse you got out there. Where'd you get it?"

"It was at the hitch rack when I broke out." She grinned at him. "I hate to tell you. But I didn't ask the owner permission to borrow it."

Pleased, Sutter lay back on his bunk and crossed his arms under his head. "I can see you now on that horse, lighting out. Like someone lit a firecracker under you. Must've been quite a sight."

Mary Lou was at the table, sorting out the contents of the two saddlebags. Sutter watched her placing the cans of beans to one side, then the cans of salt pork, and after that the sack of sugar and the tins of condensed milk. There was plenty of hardtack, too, he noticed.

Abruptly, he sat up.

"Where'd you get all them provisions?"

"They were in the saddlebags."

"You mean they were already on the horse when you took it?"

"That's what I said."

"All that food just waitin' in the saddlebags, like the horse waitin' at the hitch rack."

"What are you drivin' at, Carl?"

Carl stood up and walked over to her; without warning, he snatched the Colt out of her belt.

"Hey!" Mary Lou cried, stepping back from the table.

"You say you took this gun from the deputy?"

"That's right. He was drunk."

Carl stepped back, raised the gun and fired point-blank at Mary Lou. She screamed, staggered back—then realized he had missed.

"Carl!" she cried, terrified.

He fired again, the cabin shuddering from the detonation. Again without visible effect. This time there could be no doubt. The revolver contained only blanks. Flinging the gun to the floor, Carl strode to the door and flung it open to stare down the slope at the timber patching the slope beyond. The sun was behind the mountains now and dusk was filling the valley rapidly, flowing in like smoke. He caught no movement in the timber and saw nothing on the slope, but that didn't mean a damn thing.

He flung around in the open doorway to stare back in at her. His grin was gone now. A furious contempt blazed in his eyes.

"You dumb female! You know what you done?"

She knew all right. Shaking her head in disbelief, she slumped into a chair at the table.

Slamming the door shut, he strode over and glared down at her. "They *let* you out! It was a trick! They wanted me, so they let you out—and you've led them here to me. They're out there now, waiting for me!"

Tears streamed down her face. She lifted it to his. "You mean for *us*, Carl."

"Hell, it ain't you they want! You didn't kill no one!"

"But I'm with you now, Carl. I'll never leave you. Together we can shoot our way out of this!"

"Not with them blanks, we can't."

"We'll pull out tonight. We won't wait. We can lose them easy in this country."

His lip curled in contempt. "You mean we won't have no play time tonight?"

"You know what I mean."

He shook his head resolutely. "You're bad luck, Mary Lou. A Jonah. Since I joined up with you, I ain't been seein' clear. It's that dark patch between your legs. It done blinded me. But no more. I'm leaving you behind, Mary Lou."

"Please, Carl. Don't leave me here. Take me with you!"

"Sorry, Mary Lou. I'm all packed and ready to light out. I got to travel fast. Can't do that with a woman taggin' along. Only good thing is you brought me a fresh horse."

She jumped to her feet. "Carl! Please! Don't talk like that!"

"Okay. I won't say another word."

He drew his own weapon, cocked it, and fired into Mary Lou.

She felt the awful punch as the slug entered her belly. The next thing she knew her back had slammed into the wall and her knees were turning to jelly as she slid to the floor. The cabin's interior spun about her head. Looking up, she saw Carl had moved closer and was standing over her, taking aim again. She couldn't believe this was happening to her. Carl's finger tightened on the trigger and the world exploded into fire.

But only for a moment.

• • •

"You hear that?" Billings said.

"Wait!" Longarm told him, holding up his hand.

Another shot came from the cabin above them. Two shots. What the hell was going on? A lovers' quarrel?

The two men were crouched behind a pile of boulders at the foot of the slope. They had made a circuit of the valley in order to get this close without detection. The cabin was hidden from view, well back behind the brow of the hill.

Two more shots echoed dimly. To Longarm, these sounded ominously louder, more final.

"I think I know what happened," he told Billings.

"What?"

"Sutter found out that Colt Mary Lou was carrying was loaded with blanks. He knows we're out here now, and he's finished Mary Lou off for letting herself be suckered like that."

"Jesus, Long."

"Hell, he's mean enough. The only other explanation is the two of them are having target practice in a cabin not much bigger than an outhouse."

Billings peered up the darkening slope. "That poor, stupid little witch."

"We better get on up there, before Sutter decides to light out."

But the dusk rapidly turned to darkness, making their progress up the steep, shale-covered slope slow and troublesome. Besides, they had to move cautiously; they didn't know for sure that Sutter might not be somewhere above them in the enshrouding darkness, waiting for them to poke their heads up.

They were only halfway up the slope when the sudden thunder of hoofs sounded above them. Their first thought was that Sutter was charging down the slope at them. They flung themselves to the ground, guns cocked, and waited. But almost at once the hoofbeats faded.

Longarm turned to look over at Billings. "The sonof-abitch has another way off this slope."

"We should've figured that."

The two men stood up. Longarm started up the slope.

"Guess we better see what that bastard left for us," he said.

Billings was no more anxious than Longarm to inspect Sutter's cabin. In gloomy silence, the two men trudged up the slope and pushed open the cabin door and stepped inside.

Chapter 12

They spent little time in the cabin, and left it in flames, Mary Lou still inside—the best way to handle it, they figured. The trail Sutter used took them close to the rock face for a quarter of a mile, then down a narrow game trail that led to the valley floor a mile farther on. They stayed on the trail throughout the night and found themselves able to follow easily the fleeing Sutter's tracks.

Dismounting alongside a shallow, pebbled stream to water their horses, Longarm hunkered down beside Sutter's tracks. After a look, he straightened.

"Hey, Billings. Get over here."

Stoppering his canteen, Billings ambled over. "What's up?"

"Take a look at those tracks."

Billings hunkered down beside them. His appraisal was as swift as Longarm's. He stood up.

"The damn fool. He took Mary Lou's horse."

"He probably figured it would be a lot stronger than his own."

"And maybe it was. But not for long, not at the rate he's pushing it. Notice anything else about these here tracks?"

"Sure. They're deep."

"You got an explanation for that?"

"This ground is soft."

"It ain't that soft. Let's take a look back here."

With Billings in the lead, the two men walked back along the trail, their eyes focused on the tracks left by Sutter's horse. It was soon obvious that Sutter's tracks were consistently deeper. His horse was carrying an unusually heavy load.

"Hell, Sutter's still carrying gold."

"Sure. The clerk at the Wells Fargo Express office told me the mine owners figured they were still out a couple of thousand, at least. We hadn't got it all at the Wills's ranch, and of course if Mary Lou knew about it, she wasn't about to mention it."

They returned to their horses, mounted up, and continued on after the fleeing Sutter.

About noon they came out onto a small, sunlit upland park. The ground held a light cover of sparse, burnt-out pasture grass and a few weeds that had already gone to seed. Despite the recent thunderstorms and cloudbursts, the surface was well drained, and the hoofprints left by Sutter's weary horse no longer sank so deeply into the turf. But from the length of the animal's stride, it was clear Sutter was pushing his mount too hard.

A stream appeared off to their right, cutting a swift,

nearly straight channel through the high parkland. Billings swung his mount toward it, Longarm following.

"Time to water the horses," he said, "and rest up some ourselves."

They were both very weary men. But Billings still seemed to have an edge on Longarm. Where in the hell Billings got his prodigious energy, Longarm had no idea. But one thing was for sure: Billy Vail had sure as hell taught the man well. If Vail could see Billings tracking Sutter, he would be mighty proud.

When they reached the stream, they dismounted, off-saddled their horses and led them to the edge of the stream, making sure they did not gulp down the water too quickly. They didn't. As usual, the horses had more sense than most humans. After slaking their own thirst, the two men filled their canteens, then leaned back against a smooth-sided boulder on the stream bank. Longarm had filled the crown of his Stetson and brought it with him over to the boulder. Once he got himself comfortable, he emptied the icy water over his head, then snugged the damp hat down securely. He shivered deliciously.

Billings observed all this without comment.

Longarm took out two cheroots and offered one to the sheriff. With a grunt of thanks, Billings took it and allowed Longarm to light it for him. Once the two men got their cheroots drawing well, Longarm said, "I noticed something."

"Did you now?"

"Yep. Sutter knows for sure he's being followed."

"What makes you say that?"

"His tracks. They pause at this stream, then continue

on. Same pace. The man's in a big hurry. He doesn't have any imagination."

Billings smiled, pleased to hear Longarm referring to his earlier lecture on the criminal mind's lack of imagination.

"Yep," he said. "Sutter has no imagination at all. He can't see beyond his nose. A horse can carry a man so far, then it will drop. Carrying a man *and* gold is a whole new kettle of fish, and this fool Sutter can't see that. The gold will bring him down. As I always knew it would. It's too damned heavy, gold is, but no outlaw ever thinks of what that heft can do to a man on the run. Just a pure and simple lack of imagination."

"Is that how it was with you?"

"You mean in North Dakota?"

"Yes."

"Let me tell you about that heist. The truth is I was the only one in that gang that *did* have any imagination. The day before we were to take that bank, I rode in with Willy Starrett to look the town over. What I saw, or felt, made the hair stand up on the back of my neck."

"How come?"

"I could tell that everyone in that town knew who we were and what we were planning to do the next morning."

"They *knew*?"

"Everything."

"Who was it gave you away?"

"Looking back, I figure it was the four members of our gang who cased the town a couple of weeks before. I'm almost certain of it. These townsmen were tough, hard-drinking ploughmen and roustabouts, and they had their eyes open. One look at those four men poking

168

around and they knew what was coming. So they loaded their weapons and kept them handy, waiting for us to show. And that's what I could feel as I rode down Main Street with Willy that day. I could feel their eyes on the back of my neck. I could see the steel glint in their eyes as we rode past the bank. I could feel them waiting for me or Willy to make any sudden move."

"Then why'd you go ahead and try to rob it?"

"I didn't. The gang did."

"Didn't you try to warn them?"

"Of course I did."

"They wouldn't listen, you mean."

"Wouldn't listen? They thought I was crazy. That I had a yellow streak running clear down to my asshole. They threatened me, told me there was no way they were going to let me run out on them, and when that didn't work, they left me behind—with a warning that if they ever caught sight of me again, they'd feed me to the wolves. And I believed them."

"What you're saying is you didn't take part in that robbery."

"You don't have to believe me. And no jury probably would. But the pure and simple truth of it is I was too dad-blamed scared to take part in that robbery."

"Before he died, one of the gang members swore you took part."

Billings smiled sardonically. "I'll bet that was Willy. He hated my guts for pulling out. He probably figured I was the one who warned the townsmen. I can't really blame him. I don't suppose any one of them could figure out a better explanation for what happened. They just didn't have any—"

"Imagination," Longarm finished.

"That's the way I see it."

"And that explains to me why you took this job as sheriff at Rimrock. Since you didn't take part in the robbery, you didn't think anyone was looking for you."

Billings simply nodded.

"Hell, Billings, looks to me like that's one time when *you* lacked imagination."

Billings laughed. It was a loud, hearty laugh. He saw clearly the joke on himself this time and enjoyed it as much as Longarm.

"Of course, I'm still going to have to bring you in," Longarm explained. "But once you're cleared, you'll be a free man, and you can go back to your job as sheriff of Rimrock."

"You believe that, do you?"

"Of course."

"Now you're the one with no imagination, Long. After all these years, who's going to clear my name? What's my word against that of a dying outlaw? The way most juries see it, no man staring at the fires of hell would choose such a time to lie."

Longarm saw the sheriff's point. But he also knew he had no alternative. He had done what Billy Vail asked: he had checked to make sure that Billings was, in fact, a member of the gang that robbed that North Dakota bank. And that Longarm had established without any doubt.

"You're still going to take me in, aren't you?" Billings said.

"I don't have any choice."

"Good," Billings said, smiling. "I think Billy Vail would be proud of you. If he ain't already."

• • •

Riding across a flat a couple of hours later, they caught sight of a rider cresting a distant ridge about a mile ahead of them. For an instant, horse and rider stood out sharply against the horizon. The rider turned in his saddle, sunlight glinting off his side arm. Then he was gone.

"He saw us," Longarm said.

"Yep," Billings acknowledged.

"That means he'll be waiting for us up ahead somewhere."

"That's what I'd do if I were him. Now he knows we're that close to him."

Less than an hour later, Billings, riding ahead of Longarm, suddenly pulled up and dismounted to examine fresh tracks. They were a few miles into a steep-sided canyon, its floor littered with boulders, some of which were as big as houses. Longarm dismounted as Billings followed the tracks into a stand of scrub pine growing close along the base of the canyon wall.

When Longarm overtook the sheriff, the man was standing before a large round boulder lodged flush against the canyon wall. An attempt had been made to brush away the tracks around it with a pine branch, but the effort had been halfhearted at best.

Arms akimbo, Billings stared for a while at the boulder, then turned to Longarm. "There's a tree branch back there along the trail. We'll need it to pry up this boulder."

"You expecting to find buried treasure?"

"No, buried gold."

Longarm went after the tree branch and lugged it back to the boulder. In the meantime, Billings had dug out a small tunnel with his hands, and it was into this opening the two of them thrust the heavy end of the branch.

"Looks like it's already been used," Longarm said, noting a few spots where small branches had recently been snapped off.

"And most likely for the same purpose."

They thrust the end of the branch in still farther under the boulder. When it was in far enough, both men put their shoulders under the branch, and flexing their knees, heaved upward. Straining, they could see the dim shine of the leather saddlebags tucked into a hollowed-out depression.

"I'll hold the branch," Billings told Longarm. "See if you can reach in there and pull them bags out."

Longarm eased the branch down farther onto Billings's shoulder. When the man had rooted his feet solidly into the sand, he nodded to Longarm. Longarm dropped his hat beside the boulder, went down on his knees, and reached in as far as he could under the boulder. As he did so, the branch shifted slightly, the boulder moving with it. Longarm felt cold sweat standing out on his forehead. If the sheriff wanted to, he could see to it that he did not have to make that long trip back to Denver with Longarm. He could finish Longarm off right here. Longarm glanced back. The sheriff's straining face was getting darker.

"Hurry it up, for Christ's sake," Billings told him. "We ain't got all day."

Longarm turned back around and, crouching still lower, thrust his head and shoulders all the way in under the boulder. Particles of sand from its damp underside dropped down his neck; some fell on his face. He had to blink to clear the gritty sand out of his eyes. Reaching in deeper, he managed to close his right hand around the lip of the nearest saddlebag. As he pulled it out, the gold in it made a furrow in the sandy soil. Dragging it out past him, he turned about and reached in for the other one.

He had to go deeper this time. Bracing his knees on the soil, he wriggled himself further in. When he had a firm grip on the second saddlebag, he backed out, aware as he did so that his breath was coming in short gasps while sweat poured off his forehead and down his back.

As soon as he was out from under the boulder, Billings stepped back and released the branch. The boulder slammed down like some giant turtle back, its edges digging into the soft ground. Blowing out his cheeks, Longarm turned to face Billings.

But the man was not even looking at him. He was already down on one knee, opening the saddlebags. Watching Billings, Longarm realized that he had never been in any danger; Tom Billings would never have let that boulder fall no matter what advantage he might gain as a result.

Picking up his hat, Longarm brushed himself off, then hunkered down beside Billings. The sheriff was counting out the leather pouches. Opening one, he poured out the coins. They gleamed like brilliant dandelions in the sunlight.

"Most of it's here," Billings said after a cursory count. He placed the coins back in the pouch and tied the drawstring, then placed the pouch back into the saddlebag. "We can just shove these bags behind the boulder and pick them up on the way back."

That made sense. Their own horses were too far gone to keep up the chase and still haul all this gold. When

Billings finished refilling and tying up the saddlebags, he walked over and dropped them down behind the boulder. Joining Longarm, he turned and glanced back at the boulder, a frown on his face.

"What I'd like to know," he said, "is how in the hell Sutter was able to heave that boulder up and at the same time dig a hole under it for them saddlebags."

Longarm had already been trying to figure out the same thing, and was pretty sure he had found out how Sutter had managed it. "Come over here," he told Billings.

Billings followed Longarm a few feet further along the canyon wall, where Longarm pointed out to him the depression that followed along the base of the canyon wall.

"He dug the hole over there first," Longarm suggested, "dumped the saddlebags into it, then used that branch to manhandle the boulder along the ground onto them."

Billings bent for a moment to inspect the slicked ground. Chuckling, he straightened. "That's how he did it, all right. Pretty damn clever."

"Yeah. Real clever."

Longarm's tone caused Billings to look more closely at him. At once he burst into a laugh. "Why, Deputy, what's the matter? Did you maybe get a little nervous under that rock?"

Longarm smiled ruefully. "Hell, no more so than I would've hanging from a lightning rod in a thunderstorm."

Chuckling, Billings led the way out of the scrub pine and mounted up. Turning in his saddle to address Longarm, he said, "Sutter's getting smart, looks like. He's lightening his mount's load."

"It's too late," Longarm said, pulling his horse around.

"Why do you say that?"

"When a man like Sutter notices his horse laboring, it's already too late."

Billings smiled. "That's just about what I was thinking."

Two miles farther on, Longarm found himself peering warily at the canyon floor ahead of him. Both canyon walls had long since eroded away into a series of broken towers looming high above the valley floor, every crag and niche an ideal spot for ambush. Carl Sutter had already killed at least two men. He might have limited imagination when it came to horses and people, but there was little evidence that this failing in any way hampered his aim.

Longarm reined in his horse. Billings did the same.

"What is it?" Billings asked. "You see anything?"

"Nope. But that don't mean we shouldn't be ready for anything."

"What do you want to do?"

"I'll go ahead. You keep back. No sense in giving Sutter two good targets at the same time. If he fires on me, I'll break for the canyon wall and you cover me."

"You figure he's close by?"

"We'll know for sure when we find his dead horse."

Billings said nothing more and let Longarm ride on a good twenty yards ahead of him. A half a mile farther on, Longarm pulled up and pointed to the trail ahead. Billings rode up to join him and the two found themselves peering at what remained of a dead horse. It was about two hundred yards farther on, lying smack in the middle of the trail. It reminded Longarm of a woman's oversized leather purse gleaming in the sun. Two buzzards were already feeding on the corpse and two more were rocking slightly in the updraft as they readied themselves to drop.

"We better separate," Longarm said. "Right now."

The sharp crack of a rifle echoed through the canyon. As the round ricocheted off a rock behind him, Longarm grabbed his rifle and hurled himself from his saddle. He landed running and headed for a huge boulder close against the canyon wall. As he crouched behind it, another round whanged off the top of the boulder. A second later, Billings pulled up beside him.

"Try to draw his fire," Longarm said. "I want to see where the sonofabitch is."

"Which way you going?"

"I'll make for that rise near the cliff face."

Billings nodded and poked his head out carefully, his eyes searching the canyon's broken wall. "Now!"

Longarm ran out from behind the boulder. Digging hard, he scrambled up the embankment. Loose gravel and broken plates of shale and other debris made the footing particularly treacherous. He went to his knees twice, but kept going. He was heading for a small clump of pine halfway up and was almost to it when Sutter opened up on him, his rapid fire sending geysers of sand and stone into the air all around him.

Billings returned Sutter's fire from below and Sutter's rifle went silent. Longarm plunged into the pines and flattened himself behind a tree. Peering down at Billings, he shouted, "Where is he?"

"On that ledge," Billings shouted back, pointing.

"All right. Come ahead!"

Billings broke from behind the boulder and plunged up the slope toward him, while Longarm kept his rifle trained on the ledge. It was an eagle's nest set high above the canyon floor and boasted an unobstructed view of the canyon below.

Billings was halfway up the slope when Sutter's head and shoulders appeared and Longarm caught the gleam of his rifle barrel. Longarm squeezed off two quick shots and Sutter ducked back out of sight. A moment later, Billings plunged into the pines and slumped down beside Longarm. He was breathing heavily and his knees looked about as banged up as Longarm's.

"Now what?" Billings demanded, peering across at the ledge.

Longarm took a while before answering. He was studying the canyon wall a little farther down. "There's a game trail across the canyon," he pointed out. "It just might lead around behind that ledge."

"You mean you're going to try to make it back across that open canyon floor?"

"I'll keep my head down."

"It's your ass he'll be aiming at."

"I'm counting on you to cover me."

"This is a real long shot, Deputy."

"You got any better ideas?"

"Nope."

"Keep the sonofabitch busy. That's all I ask."

Billings nodded, his eyes on the ledge, and cranked a fresh cartridge into his rifle's firing chamber. Longarm broke from the pines, plunged recklessly back down the slope and hit the canyon floor running full stride. Sutter

177

had already opened up, the rounds whining uncomfortably close. From the slope behind Longarm came Billings's answering fire. It was a steady enough fusilade and did the trick. Sutter's fire diminished in volume, then stopped entirely. A moment later Longarm reached the canyon wall. Keeping close in under it, he ran down the canyon until he came to the game trail. It had looked negotiable enough from the pines. But moving up its narrow path across the steep cliff wall, Longarm realized he had a difficult climb ahead of him.

But it took him to where he wanted to go, a flat slablike rock from which he could fire down upon the ledge where Sutter crouched. Though Sutter was not visible at the moment, Longarm poured down a steady fire, hoping the ricocheting bullets would intimidate Sutter long enough to prevent him from cutting down Billings.

Longarm saw Billings plunge down the slope and dart across the canyon, then disappear in the rocks beneath him. Longarm stopped firing at the ledge and waited for Sutter to reappear. A minute, then another minute passed, and Longarm was still waiting. Abruptly, he swore aloud in a fury at his own stupidity. Carl Sutter was no longer on that ledge beneath him!

So where the hell was he?

A quiet, mean chuckle—and the sound of a Colt being thumb-cocked—came from behind him. Longarm whirled. A grinning Carl Sutter was standing behind him on the edge of the rock, his Colt leveled on Longarm's gut.

Someone blew a hole in Sutter's back.

Sutter staggered forward, reached out blindly, then plunged awkwardly past Longarm and dropped from sight. Longarm peered over and saw Sutter's body bounce off two ledges, then disappear into a tangle of rocks and brush on the canyon floor.

Longarm turned to see Sheriff Billings step out from behind a rock, his rifle at the ready, its muzzle leveled on Longarm, his eyes grim.

"This is good-bye, Deputy," he said. "You won't be taking me back to Denver."

"You mean you aren't going to stay and let me thank you?"

"I'd appreciate it if you'd give my regards to Billy. Tell him I've got me a well-stocked horse ranch, so he shouldn't worry none."

"I'll tell him."

"And if he ever wants to latch on to some fine horse-flesh, he could do worse than visit the Twin Pines."

"Twin Pines?"

"It's not a town, but Billy will know what I mean."

"I'll tell him."

"I'd like a couple of hours, Long."

"You got it."

Billings stepped off the ledge and disappeared down the slope. A moment later Longarm heard the clatter of his horse's hooves. As they faded, Longarm sat down on the edge of the rock and took from his inside jacket pocket the arrest warrant Billy Vail had given him. He tore it up and tossed it into the canyon, then shucked his hat back off his head and lit up a fresh cheroot.

Chapter 13

Billy Vail ducked into the booth and ordered a whiskey and water from the waiter, who had hurried over as soon as Vail entered. They were in the Windsor Hotel's saloon. Longarm had not yet had a chance to visit his digs on the other side of Colfax Avenue.

"I got your message," Vail said. "When did you get in?"

"An hour ago."

Vail's drink arrived. He paid for it, then looked across at Longarm. "Well? How'd it go?"

"It's a long story."

"I got all night."

Longarm's account didn't take that long, and when he finished, Billy Vail leaned back in his seat. After a moment, he said, "And you say there was nothing taken from them saddlebags?"

"Not from what that Wells Fargo clerk in Mountain

City told me after he finished toting it all up. It was all there."

"Tom could have taken both saddlebags easy enough."

"He could have."

"And you believe his story. That he pulled out of that North Dakota heist because he got cold feet."

"No, because he had good sense."

Billy said nothing for a moment, then nodded. "I agree. The Tom Billings I remember had plenty of good sense. Like he says, imagination. I just don't see how he could've let himself join up with a gang like that."

"Not all of us are perfect, Billy."

"Anyway, that stage heist was foiled, the miners got their gold, and Wells Fargo doesn't have Carl Sutter to worry about anymore."

"That's about the size of it, Chief."

"We don't need to talk about Tom Billings after this, Longarm. As far as anyone in the office knows, it was Carl Sutter I sent you after, and you were good enough to nail him. Now that Tom knows the government's tied him in with that heist, he'll have sense enough to change his name, or at least quit taking any more jobs as sheriff. At any rate, my report to Washington ought to cool things off for him." Vail's gaze lifted past Longarm, his eyes reflective. "Twin Pines, huh?"

"Where might that be, Chief?"

"I won't burden you with such knowledge, Longarm. All I can say is Tom's picked the one spot I'd have picked myself."

"Then maybe you'll visit him someday."

"Maybe. If I ever kick this town's dust from my boots."

Billy Vail finished his drink, scooted out of the booth and slapped Longarm affectionately on the shoulder. "Good night, Longarm. Glad to have you back. Take tomorrow off."

"Thanks, Chief."

As Billy Vail left, Longarm rested his head back against the booth's leather seat and lifted in salute his glass of Maryland rye.

"Here's to you, Tom Billings," he murmured softly, "wherever you are. Good luck."

Watch for

LONGARM AND THE DAY OF DEATH

one hundred twenty-eighth novel in the bold
LONGARM series from Jove

coming in August!

Explore the exciting Old West with one of the men who made it wild!

Check book(s). Fill out coupon. Send to:

BERKLEY PUBLISHING GROUP
390 Murray Hill Pkwy., Dept. B
East Rutherford, NJ 07073

NAME_____

ADDRESS_____

CITY_____

STATE_____ ZIP _____

**PLEASE ALLOW 6 WEEKS FOR DELIVERY.
PRICES ARE SUBJECT TO CHANGE
WITHOUT NOTICE.**

POSTAGE AND HANDLING:
$1.00 for one book, 25¢ for each additional. Do not exceed $3.50.

BOOK TOTAL	$ _____
POSTAGE & HANDLING	$ _____
APPLICABLE SALES TAX
(CA, NJ, NY, PA)	$ _____
TOTAL AMOUNT DUE	$ _____

PAYABLE IN US FUNDS.
(No cash orders accepted.)

201